GRAVEPYRES SCHOOL FOR THE RECENTLY DECEASED

GRAVEPYRES SCHOOL FOR THE RECENTLY DECEASED

Anita Roy

To Paddy

Happy Reading!

Anita

August '22

RED PANDA

First published by Red Panda, an imprint of Westland Publications Private Limited, in 2020

1st Floor, A Block, East Wing, Plot No. 40, SP Infocity, Dr MGR Salai, Perungudi, Kandanchavadi, Chennai 600096

Westland, the Westland logo, Red Panda and the Red Panda logo are the trademarks of Westland Publications Private Limited, or its affiliates.

Copyright © Anita Roy, 2020

ISBN: 9789389152418

10 9 8 7 6 5 4 3 2 1

This is a work of fiction. Names, characters, organisations, places, events and incidents are either products of the author's imagination or used fictitiously.

Typeset by SÜRYA, New Delhi
Printed at Thomson Press (India) Ltd.

for Roshan
Dispeller of Darkness

'**Y**ou're late.'

The small girl who made this pronouncement stood in front of Jose with her arms crossed and a look of deep disapproval on her face. The bewilderment on his didn't seem to affect her in the slightest.

Jose, on the other hand, was completely confused. For a start, he appeared to be standing up, when seconds ago he was lying down. He was outdoors standing on a misty hillside, on short, rough grass, when he ought to have been inside, tucked up safely in his bed. And instead of his parents' warm and familiar faces, he was confronted with this rather fierce little girl who he'd never set eyes on in his life.

'What?' he said.

'Pardon,' she said.

'What?'

This conversation was not going well.

'*Pardon*,' she said. 'You shouldn't keep going whatwhatwhat all the time. It's very rude.'

'I...'

'Never mind,' she interrupted – rather rudely, Jose thought – and turned to go. She set off up a short slope towards a large wooden door that lay deep set into an imposing stone wall. She stood on tiptoe to grasp a large metal ring in its centre, and pulled down to lift the latch. Then she turned around and leaned her back against the door to push it open. Jose hadn't moved an inch from where he stood. The girl paused in her efforts and rolled her eyes at him.

'Help?' she said, and beckoned.

'Oh,' said Jose, and went over to add his weight to the door.

Between the two of them, they managed to get it to open just enough to allow them through. The girl suddenly flashed him a grin.

'Thanks,' she said. 'I'm Mishi, by the way.'

'I'm Jose,' said Jose. 'Where am I?'

The little girl rolled her eyes at this. 'Here of course,' she said, with an impish grin. She grabbed his hand and pulled him through the doorway. 'We're here!'

'Here' turned out to be a wide courtyard flanked on all sides by the stone walls of a what looked to Jose like some sort of monastery. In the middle of the courtyard stood an ancient, gnarled tree. Its massive trunk was massive and deeply fissured, deformed with bulges and boles, and the reddish-brown bark stood out in plates. Its branches twisted and turned as though clawing their way upwards to the leaden, grey sky.

The walls of the buildings leaned away from the courtyard slightly as they rose up. Narrow windows, balustrades and balconies were dotted here and there, each topped with a red-tiled roof that tilted up at the ends like the tip of a dragon's tail, and brightly painted. Mishi headed for a doorway on the other side of the courtyard which, like the window frames, was carved and painted with intricate designs. Hurrying after her, Jose glanced nervously at the winged serpents, grimacing leopards, conch shells licked with flames, spiralling clouds and many-petalled lotus flowers that wound their way up the columns on either side like leaves and tendrils around a tree. Across the top of the door, words were chiselled into the stone:

Gravepyres School for the Recently Deceased

Jose barely had time to register them as he ran after Mishi, who had already disappeared inside.

As his eyes adjusted to the gloom, he found himself in a cavernous entrance hall. It was like stepping into a cathedral, high and arched and silent. The sound of the children's footsteps seemed to be absorbed by the thick stone walls as though they mopped up sound like a sponge.

Across the hallway, along a corridor, through
another, up one flight of stairs and down again, Jose
struggled to keep up with the little figure who skip-
hopped ahead of him. I must be asleep, he thought
to himself. That's the only explanation: it's one of
those vivid dreams that seems so real, and then you
wake up and find yourself at home in bed, and it's
all right and nothing has changed. The problem was
that it didn't feel like a dream at all: in fact, Jose was
feeling more awake than he had in a long time. His
senses were sharp and keen, his body felt agile and
light – he'd almost forgotten what it was like to be
able to move about so easily, so painlessly, and not
like he was tethered to his inert torso and heavy
limbs. He had got used to feeling that his body was
a dead weight to be dragged along the seabed, not a
jaunty sailboat skipping along the surface.

He put on a burst of speed as he rounded the
corner. Mishi was skipping along ahead of him,
her bare legs peeking out from under her tunic.
Behind the doors that they passed on either side of
the corridor, Jose could occasionally make out the
murmur of voices. It sounded like lessons were going
on – but the sounds were muffled and he couldn't
make out any words.

Just then Mishi and Jose walked past a large
mirror suspended on a big brass chain from the walls
of the corridor. Mishi glanced up and gave a little
shriek.

'What?' said Jose, spooked.

Mishi just pointed at their reflection. A young girl of six or seven, with a pageboy haircut and bright black eyes and dressed in an orange-brown tunic down to her knees stared back down at them. And next to her, a lad with tousled dark brown hair and thick black eyebrows stood in barefeet, wearing pyjamas, and looking a bit lost. On his shirt was a faded image of the Incredible Hulk smashing through a building, and the trousers – now showing a few inches of ankle, given his recent growth spurt – were a matching shade of green. A birthday present from his mother two years ago, Jose remembered, now worn to a comfortable softness.

'You can't go in like *that*,' said Mishi. 'You need some *proper* clothes. This way.'

She turned on her heels and led him back the way they'd come, and then turned down a long, low tunnel-like opening into a small room, where a bald, round-faced nun wearing wire-rimmed glasses was sitting at a desk, a newspaper open in front of her, thoughtfully sucking the end of a pencil. She looked up as they came in.

'Oh hello, Mishi,' said the nun. 'Another one, then?'

'Yes,' she replied. 'Just *look* at him.'

'Hmmm. We'll have to do something about that.'

Jose thought it was very rude to talk about him as though he wasn't there. 'I don't...' he began, but the nun had already turned away and was sorting through piles of cloth stacked on the shelves behind her, muttering to herself.

'Shrouds, vestments, winding sheet... ah, here we are. Robes – transitioner. Bit skinny isn't he? Size eight should do it, I think. He'll need a belt. Here.'

She handed Jose a pile of cloth, with a rope belt coiled on top, and gestured towards a curtain off to one side.

'You can change in there.'

There was no room for argument, so Jose did as he was told. I can always get my clothes back later, he thought, when it's time to go back.

He came out, feeling rather foolish with his bare legs sticking out from under the long orange tunic. The nun told him to take off his shoes, and handed him a pair of soft leather sandals. Then she bundled up Jose's clothes and sneakers and headed towards a small black iron door set into the wall that hinged open from the top.

Jose hardly had time to read the sign next to it – 'Mortal Remains' – before, ignoring his sudden cry of despair, the nun chucked in his clothes and shoes, and closed the door with a clang. She pressed a button next to the door, a green light went on that said 'Incineration in progress' and with a sudden *fwhoosh,* it was all over.

'*Hey!*' Jose cried out. 'What are you doing!? Those were my... that was my...'

The nun and Mishi exchanged a look.

'Oh, don't worry,' Mishi said, 'you won't be needing them again. Come on, we have to go. Thank you, Didi.'

Mishi bowed to the nun, who bowed back, and then picked up her pencil and returned to her crossword. 'Five down, seven letters, *p*, something, *d*, something…'

II

Still smarting from the loss of his clothes, and feeling rather silly and self-conscious in his tunic, Jose followed Mishi until they came to a door. She pushed it open and beckoned Jose inside. In a large, plain room, about thirty children of various shapes and sizes were sitting cross-legged on the dark mahogany floor. In front of them were rows of long wooden benches. On a low dais at the far end of the room sat a skeletal man wrapped in yellow robes, his paper-white skin almost the same colour as the silk scarf draped around his shoulders. He was studying an enormous ledger that lay open on the low table next to him. He looked up over his half-moon glasses as Mishi and Jose came in.

'Ah, Mishi – I was wondering where you'd got to. Come in, come in. And this must be…' He trailed a long, white finger down the entries on the page, and then stopped and tapped it twice. 'Joseph Eapen Srinivas, I presume?'

Jose nodded. *How did he...?*

'Good, wonderful,' said the man. 'Now then, Meredith, if you scoot up a little, and Mishi can sit there, and Jose – next to Mishi? Yes? Good, good. Great.'

He stood up – he was tall and very, very thin. He looked so awkward and ungainly that as he got to his feet, Jose was reminded of someone struggling to unfold a deck-chair in a gale. Once he was up, the man interlaced his fingers, reversed them, palms outward, and pushed. They went off like a little volley of firecrackers. He beamed down at the children, looking highly pleased with the performance.

Addressing Jose, he said, 'I am Professor Styx, your Mathamythics teacher, as well as – I'm pleased to say – your form tutor. Any problemsworriesquestions, you come to me, yes? These, of course, are your fellow transitioners, and together we will crack the mysteries of the universe! Well, the numbers part anyway. Chalo. Let us begin.'

He twirled around and swiftly wrote on the large slate blackboard that hung from the wall, using only the bone-white tip of his index finger:

$6 + 4 =$

Jose looked from side to side. The other students – what had he called them? 'Transitioners'? – looked down at their notebooks, some scribbling frantically, others looking puzzled. One boy stared at the ceiling, his mouth slightly open.

'Anyone want to have a go?' said Professor Styx.

Surely, thought Jose, surely they can't all be that thick. I mean, anyone can answer that. Even his little sister Surya could do that sum, and she was only four.

A girl towards the front of the class tentatively raised her hand.

'Four hundred and sixteen?' she said.

Jose suppressed a snort.

'Good, good, excellent, Ruby, well done,' said Professor Styx. 'How about you, Surojit?'

A boy of about twelve looked up, startled, and scratched his cheek. 'Uh, ninety-seven? And a half?'

'Nice,' said Professor Styx. 'Anyone else?'

A few more hands went up. 'Eight thousand.' 'Fifty-two.' 'Twelve.' 'Minus fourteen.' Jose frowned. This was ridiculous.

'Ten,' he said loudly.

'Jose, would you...?' said the teacher.

'Ten,' he said, even louder. 'Six plus four equals ten.'

'Oh dear,' said Professor Styx. 'Not quite.'

Jose sat there fuming. What sort of teacher was this? Everyone knows six plus four is ten. Not nearly, not 'not quite', not more, nor less, not maybe – it just *is*. What were these idiots playing at? His ears burned with indignation.

The rest of the lesson made precisely the same amount of sense, which is to say absolutely none at all.

The next lesson was hardly any better. 'Scare Studies', so Mishi informed him, was taught by Madam Morte, the deputy deadmistress. Like Professor Styx, she was tall and thin and dressed in teacherly yellow robes. She had light grey eyes and dark red lips set in a long, pale face and a mane of salt-and-pepper hair that reached down to the waist. Her classroom was more like a cave: roughly circular, with bare stone walls. A round opening in the roof let in a shaft of light, creating a puddle of brightness on the floor in the middle. As she paced around amongst the children, who sat in concentric rings around the sides of the room, her robes flashed – now dark and then bright – like an actor stepping from the spotlight into the shadows and back again.

Jose picked what he hoped was the darkest spot in the room, and prayed fervently that she wouldn't notice him. *Go with it, go with it, wake up, wake up, you're at home, you're asleep, this is not happening, it's not real,* the thoughts buzzed around his head like flies.

'*Mister* Srinivas.' The teacher's voice cut through his thoughts as sharp as a scissor snip. 'I realise this is your first day, but I suggest you start as you mean to go on. With a little *attention.*'

There was a smattering of giggles, quickly silenced as she raked the children with an icy stare. 'That goes for all of you.' She put a cloth shoulder-bag down on the floor next to Jose. 'Books, paper, pencils,' she said shortly and then resumed her pacing. 'Now then,' she said, raising her voice. 'Scaring requires discipline. Concentration. You must study hard, and practice harder. And even then,' she looked pointedly at a kid in the third row who was carefully excavating something from deep inside his nose, 'some of you will never master the Art. For now, turn to page 18 of your textbooks and revise the section on Churails, taking notes on Backwards Feet and General Ghastliness.'

Following the others' lead, Jose took out a large textbook from the bag Madame Morte had given him, along with a notebook and a small, brightly woven pencil case. He balanced the book on his knees. *Elementary Scarification Level 1*, it said on the cover. He turned to page 18 and began to read.

Distant cousins of the Bulgarian veshtitsi and the éguï of Japan, churails are endemic to the Indian subcontinent, and range as far as Nepal and parts of Ladakh. Their natural habitat is mixed sal woodland, although they are frequently found in mangrove swamps and temperate upland forests. Churails are largely nocturnal, coming out at dusk to feed, particularly along roadsides

and well-trodden footpaths on the outskirts of
villages, where they can often be found roosting in
the branches of the peepul tree (*Ficus religiosa*).
Churails are allergic to neem (*Azadirachta indica*),
which causes them to wilt and brings them out in
a rash.

The text carried on in this vein for several pages,
and was illustrated with an engraving of a hideous
hag-like creature sitting on the lower branch of a tree
and dangling its feet (backwards, ending in claw-like
toenails) over the head of a hapless goatherd passing
underneath. By the time he'd finished reading, Jose's
expression was not very different from the hapless
goatherd's: round-eyed and mildly idiotic.

Finally, Madam Morte cleared her throat and
folded her hands together. The children closed their
books.

'Theory, children, will only take you so far,' she
said briskly, 'so we will spend the rest of the period
on Practicals.' She steepled her fingers together
and pressed them to her lips. 'Psychic projection,
poultergeisting, astral projection and so on are all
skills to be acquired at far, far advanced levels,' and
here she sort of pushed herself out of her own body,
like someone squeezing a flannel, and reappeared in a
twisting unravel on the other side of the cave. There
was a low murmur of appreciation from the class at
such casual artistry. Madame Morte smoothed her

hair in place and carried on, apparently unconcerned. 'However, we shall start today with the basics: Going Woo. Who would like to start?' A number of hands shot up.

One after the other, the children stood up and hooted until the room echoed like a trainful of owls going through a tunnel. Then it was his turn.

Thirty heads swivelled around to look at him. Jose got to his feet unsteadily. He pushed out his lips, made a round mouth, and managed a hopeful little 'ooh?'

The rest of the class burst out laughing, the loudest guffaws of all coming from Mishi, who was sitting on the other side of the circle from him. He scowled at her and sat down, tugging his hair over his eyes. Madam Morte sternly shushed the rest of the children. 'Well now, Joseph,' she said, not unkindly, 'since you're new here, you'll just have to work that bit harder, won't you? Now, suck in the tummy, open out the chest, and...' Her eyes bugged out, her mouth sagged and distended like a water balloon, and she let out a howling wail that made every single one of Jose's hairs stand up straight. He looked like he'd been electrocuted. Mishi gave him a sideways glance as if to say, 'See? *That's* how to do it.' And Jose wanted the earth to swallow him up. Only – well, maybe it already had...

At the end of the lesson, Mishi came over to Jose

and said with disarming honesty, 'You're really bad at going woo, aren't you?'

Jose nodded morosely.

'Never mind.' She patted his hand. 'I bet you're great at Seeing.'

And with that nonsensical remark, she led him off to their next class.

There was nothing to be done but follow her meekly, so this was what he did. Unlike the Scare Studies room, this classroom was laid out like those in Jose's own school, with rows of wooden desks and chairs. Jose looked around for a spare seat, but the only one free was next to Mishi. She patted the desk and beamed at him to come over. He rolled his eyes, went over and plonked himself down, hoping against hope that his would be the last lesson of this interminable day and it would all be over soon – and he could go back home. The large, stocky figure at the front was facing away from them, looking intently up and out of the window, his hands behind his back. As the class settled down, the figure stood unmoving, obviously fascinated by whatever it was that he had spotted in the blank grey sky outside. Jose felt the nudge of an elbow in his side. 'That's Dr Chiplunker,' whispered Mishi. 'He's everso...' but what he was everso Jose never found out because at that moment Dr Chiplunker turned to face the class.

And Jose nearly fell off his chair.

He was wearing the most extraordinary spectacles that Jose had ever seen. They were – there was no other word for it – spectacular. Each lens was a different colour and the huge frames bristled with about fifty (or so it seemed) other lenses of different shapes and sizes, hinged together at the corner so they could be flipped down or lifted with the flick of a finger. Perched above the bridge of his bulbous nose was another contraption which looked, at first, like a large silver bindi. Dr Chiplunker reached up and, with a series of twists and pulls, extended it in sections until it stuck out of his forehead like a brass unicorn horn (only backwards, if you can imagine that, with the fattest end at the front). He swung it down to his right eyeglass and turned back to peer through it out of the window again. He waved a large pair of protractors around, made a swift series of scribbled calculations in the book in front of him, without looking down at all, and then collapsed the telescope back into his forehead again and glared at the children, his eyes made enormous by the extraordinary spectacles.

'Ha!' he barked. 'Is everyone here? Let's see... hmmmm.'

He called out the children's names one by one, and ticked them off in his register. When his name came, Jose put up his hand and said, 'Here, sir.'

The teacher goggled at him.

'Mmmyes. I can see that,' he said slowly. 'But are you *present*?'

'Er,' Jose patted himself down. 'I think so, sir.'

'Think so? THINK SO?' He squinted at Jose with one piercing blue eye. 'Don't you *know*?'

'Yes. I... I'm right here.'

Dr Chiplunker flipped two of the lenses over his left eye and adjusted a dial on the right. Then he stared at Jose again for a long, uncomfortable moment. 'We'll see about that,' he muttered, and made a mark in the register.

Then he slammed the book shut, which made everyone jump.

'RIGHT,' he announced, whipping out a long cane, 'let's get those eyes moving.'

Then, as though he were conducting an orchestra, Dr Chiplunker began to wave a long, tapering bamboo cane left and right and around the room. 'Left, left and right, right, right and upupup, and dowwwwwwwwwwwn, and upupup and dowwwwwwwn.' The children's eyes followed the tip of the stick. 'And spin left...' he made circles in the air with his cane, '...and right...' with fluid twists of his wrist, and all the children's eyes spun in their heads. This went on for quite a while. Jose felt like his head had been put in a blender; the colours and shapes whirled around him in a kaleidoscopic milkshake. Then, suddenly, with a final lunge, Dr Chiplunker leapt from the podium and stood stock still, the cane quivering in his outstretched hand, like a fencing master who'd just skewered his opponent through the heart.

As the room gradually stopped spinning and settled back into place, Dr Chiplunker told the children to get out their pencils. Jose fumbled around for his – his vision was still a bit wobbly and it seemed to keep twitching away from his hand. Finally, he had it firmly in his grip, and looked around to see what they should be writing on. Oddly, the other children didn't have any books or papers in front of them, but had placed their pencils neatly on their empty desks. Jose, nonplussed, did the same. He felt the beginnings of a splitting headache.

'Now,' said Dr Chiplunker, 'can you all See your pencils?'

'Yes, sir,' they chorused.

'Really?' he said, sounding deeply unconvinced and peering at them over his extraordinary specs. 'We will spend the rest of the period on "Seeing the Pencil". START!'

Jose looked at his pencil.

For a long time.

And then some more.

He wondered what his mother was doing. Maybe she was watering the plants on their balcony. Or fetching his little sister Surya from the nursery school. Or working on her computer, a mug of hot coffee at her side. Or maybe she would be sitting on the swing by the back door, reading the newspaper with their cat, Pushkin, on her lap. Or...

'*Focus!*' barked Dr Chiplunker, slamming the cane down on Jose's desk, making the pencil (and its owner) jump. He pointed to the pencil with his cane. 'Notice the tip. Is it sharp, is it blunt? How sharp? How blunt? What colour is the wood here, here – and here? See this lettering? Be with the pencil, Srinivas. *See* the pencil.'

Jose went back to 'seeing' the pencil.

It was short. It could do with sharpening. It said 'Camlin High Quality' down one side and 'HB' in gold letters near the end. And there was a thin green band that ran around it, about a centimetre from the bottom. It seemed round, but actually had – Jose turned it around, counting – four, five, six sides.

And that was it. It was just a pencil after all, an ordinary, honest-to-goodness unremarkable *pencil*.

After a little while, Jose decided that this really had to be the most boring, most pointless, most mind-numbingly dull lesson that had ever been invented in the history of the universe. While Dr Chiplunker wasn't looking, he got out his eraser and started picking it to bits underneath the desk – just for something to *do*. Time dragged on interminably and just when he'd decided that it had stopped altogether, a gong sounded.

Jose stood up, and a shower of rubber snow fell onto his shoes. Mishi fairly bounced out of the class, looking like she'd freshly bathed. 'Good, wasn't it?' she beamed at him.

'*Good*?' he spluttered. 'What was good about it?'

'Oh, you'll get used to it,' said Mishi breezily. 'You just need to practise. Seeing's pretty tough, you know.'

'No, it's really not! I mean, *everyone* can see! Unless you're blind or something,' protested Jose, but Mishi wasn't listening.

'See you in the study hall,' she said, rushing off. 'I'll save you a place.'

III

'*Homework?*' cried Jose in dismay. 'But...'

The tall girl who stood handing out papers at the door to the study hall looked at him for a long moment, one eyebrow lifted as if to say, *excuses, excuses.* She silently handed him a sheaf of papers and turned to the next in line.

The study hall was up a wide flight of wooden stairs just off the main courtyard. Outside, the light was fading, like someone had turned a dimmer switch down to its lowest setting. Candlelight flickered around the walls and along the middle of the long worktables where transitioners already had their heads bent diligently over their work. A monk – or maybe a nun, he really couldn't tell – perhaps it was the very one who'd incinerated his trousers earlier – was making his (or her) way around the room, lighting torches with a long flaming taper.

A child at the far end of one of the tables waved at him ecstatically. It seemed there was no escaping Mishi. He went over and sat down next to her. She blinked at him happily.

He put the sheets on the bench in front of him. All around him he could hear the diligent scritch-scratch of pencils on paper. Clearly, the other kids didn't seem to be bothered by the fact that 'Mathamythics' – which is what it said at the top of the worksheet – wasn't even a *thing*.

He read the first question.

How much wood would a woodchuck chuck? Give your answer in kilos per inch, and show workings, assuming that (a) a woodchuck could chuck wood and (b) the wood in question is medium-density Wellingtonia pine.

Jose groaned. His head, which already felt like a lump of lead, slumped down onto the papers. *No, no, no. This cannot be happening.*

This had been a bad day, he thought bleakly. Correction: the worst day of his whole life. A mad nun had burnt his clothes. He'd had to sit through class after bewildering class of nonsense in subjects that didn't even *exist...* and on top of everything – *homework?* It was all too much.

Jose sighed. Or, at least, he did what he could to produce a sigh, which was difficult given that he wasn't actually breathing. *Breathing… I'm not breathing? How can I not be breathing!?* He fought down the sudden surge of panic, eyes closed, head down on the table.

He felt a sharp poke on his shoulder.

'Are you alright?' Mishi whispered, wielding a pencil.

Well, there was one question he knew the answer to.

'No,' he whispered back, fiercely. 'No, I am not "alright".'

'It's okay, you can copy mine,' she said, angling her worksheet towards him slightly. 'Mind the scaretaker doesn't see,' she added indicating with her eyes the maroon-robed figure who was gliding silently along the far side, taper held aloft.

Jose glanced at her worksheet. At the top, next to 'Name' she had scrawled 'Mishi' – only the 's' was backwards. Underneath, where it said 'Date of Death' she'd put 'Larst wik.'

'Uh, thanks,' he said and pushed it back to her. To be honest, he didn't think she was going to be much help.

Jose wrote his name at the top of the paper and then hesitated, the point of his pencil hovering over 'Date of…'. Is that what he was – really? If he really, truly was dead, he wouldn't be walking around, he wouldn't be able to talk, he wouldn't be able to think or do anything – would he? He held up his hand in front of his mouth experimentally and huffed. Nothing. Not a whisper of breath escaped him. He tried again.

Then he slipped his hand beneath the fold of his tunic and held it against his chest. He sat, frozen, listening for a heartbeat. Nothing. *Nothing.* How was that possible? He fought back a rising wave of panic. If his heart were beating at all, it would have been hammering.

I've got to get home, he thought to himself. I cannot be here. This is supposed to be *home*work – work you do *at home*. I need to get back. His mother would be worried. Would she remember to feed Pushkin if he wasn't there? His dad would be frantic. And there was the science project to hand in at school – his real school, not this stupid, ridiculous, pretend one. The prospect of spending one more minute, let alone the rest of his life, learning how to 'See' or practicing 'Going Woo' or figuring out how to do Mathamythics – it was just too ghastly to contemplate.

He pushed back his chair abruptly, his mind made up.

'Where are you going?' hissed Mishi.

'I can't stay here. I'm going home.'

'What? You can't!'

'Who's going to stop me?' blurted out Jose, defiantly. The scaretaker had departed and all the other kids seemed busy with their homework. 'I'm going to get my clothes back. I've got to go...'

He started towards the door. Mishi scrambled up and caught him by the sleeve.

'You can't leave!' she said urgently, her eyes blazing. 'Nobody can.'

'Just watch me.' Jose tugged the cloth free and headed down the corridor.

'Wait!' cried Mishi. 'Wait up. Listen. Nobody goes back, understand? Nobody. Not unless you're a vulture.' She looked at him a bit uncertainly. 'You're not a vulture, are you?'

'Of course I'm not a vulture! Do I *look* like a vulture?'

Mishi looked him up and down and bit her lip. 'N... no. But it doesn't hurt to ask.'

Jose threw up his hands.

'Look. I've got to go, okay? No offence, but this place is crazy. I've got to hand in my science project tomorrow, and my mum and dad will be worried, I've got to get back h...'

Jose suddenly staggered against the wall, clutching his chest. A sharp pain, as fierce as it was fleeting, stabbed through him. The keening wail of a siren burst upon his inner ear. He was blinded by a stroboscopic glare of tubelights as he was rushed along a hospital corridor, the sound of echoing footsteps hurrying him along. His body on fire, fever raging through his veins. Snatches of voices – his father's, his mother's – coming to him like faint radio signals, bleeding away into static. His body like a burning boat, pushed out on the dark water, consuming itself in flames. Stars burst and shattered in spirals behind his eyes, racing to catch their tails. The beeping of a monitor. The cold prick of a needle, and fluid entering his arm, spreading out in icy tendrils. Then a sound. A cry that seemed to come from somewhere far beyond his mother's body, dragged from her with deep hooks from the seabed and hauled out of her lips in anguish. A sound like nothing he had ever heard emerge from human lips...

'Jack! Jack!' Mishi's voice seemed to come from far away and down a long tunnel. Her small, worried face floated before him. 'Jose,' he mumbled, 'my name is...' Then darkness bloomed around the edges of his vision, until the pool of light in the middle shrank to a puddle, then a droplet, then a pinprick. And then everything went black.

When Jose came to, he found himself lying on the stone floor of a darkened cave. In a circle around him sat eight hooded figures. They were chanting a deep, buzzing, guttural chant that rose, then fell, then rose again. From time to time, a small, high bell would ring out punctuating the chant with a clear single note, there would be a pause, and then the chanting would resume, pulsing around him, holding him as surely as salt water buoys up a float. He let himself drift away, carried by the steady rhythm of gentle waves.

After some time – he had no notion of how long – he opened his eyes. The cavern was empty save for one figure, kneeling before a small stone shrine in the darkest corner. Small oil lamps in terracotta cups added their sooty smoke to the blackened wall behind, and curls of smoke rose up from smouldering cones of incense. The figure was draped in a black cloak, on the back of which was an embroidered insignia: a snake curling in a circle, its tail in its mouth, its scales picked out in silver and crimson thread.

Jose began to sit up, and sensing his movement, the figure held up a hand. He froze. It was a skeleton hand, white bones of tarsals and metatarsals. The hand withdrew back into the folds of the cloak, and the figure resumed its muttering. With a final fling of its bony arm, the creature threw a pinch of powdery substance into the flames, causing them to crackle and fizz and send up a bloom of dark smoke to the cavern roof. Then the figure bowed down, touched its head briefly to the ground and in one smooth movement, as though drawn upward by a string, rose up.

And up.

The black figure stretched almost to the roof. Hooded and robed, the featureless shadow loomed over him, as though the cave wall had split and parted to reveal an abyss. Panicked, Jose started to edge away, scooting backwards on his bum, but as the figure approached, it seemed to shrink and diminish, its outlines becoming sharper and clearer until it coalesced into an ordinary-sized human shape before him. Then it threw back its hood to reveal the dark and strikingly long face of an old man. His close-cropped hair was pure white, as were his eyebrows, but his skin was smooth as polished ebony and unlined except, perhaps, at the edges of his deep black eyes that twinkled as though lit by starlight from within. The man smiled down at Jose.

'Joseph Eapen Srinivas,' he said, and his voice was like velvet against the skin. 'Welcome back.'

Jose stuttered, 'How... how do you know my name?'

At that, the man laughed – a loud boom that echoed around the chamber. He had the whitest teeth that Jose had ever seen. 'Well, you know, it is my business to know,' he said, seeming to find the whole situation vastly amusing. He pushed back the long sleeves of his cloak – and Jose was relieved to see that the bare bones had somehow vanished and the man's long arms now ended in quite ordinary hands with long, nimble fingers and neatly trimmed fingernails the colour of old ivory.

'But forgive me,' he went on, 'I know *your* name, of course. But have neglected to tell you mine.'

28

He walked to one side of the cave where a deep niche had been cut into the wall. From it he plucked what looked like an old-fashioned perfume bottle, filled with light blue liquid, and removed the small glass stopper.

'My name is – well, I have a number of names, and I answer to them all – but you can call me Yama. Although, honestly, and in view of (a) your tender years (b) my exalted status and (c) the fact that I hold a Ph.D. from the University of Thanatos – my special area of research being decomposition and deliquesence – I think *Professor* Yama would be a more fitting term of address. After all, I am the Deadmaster of Gravepyres School for the Recently Deceased, and that deserves at least a little bit of, ah, *gravitas*, wouldn't you say?'

All the while that he was speaking, Professor Yama was carefully letting a few drops from the bottle drip into a small terracotta dish, to which he also added other things – a couple of strands of saffron, a pinch of ash, a dribble of honey, a dash of this and a smidgen of that, including many ingredients that Jose couldn't identify. He held the little dish up to the light, added a final drop of the blue liquid and then decanted it into a small silver spoon, which he held out to Jose.

'Down in one,' he said. 'It'll do you good, I promise.'

Obediently, Jose took the spoon and put it in his mouth. It tasted utterly, spectacularly, unbelievably, stupendously *vile*. He spluttered, coughed, gagged but managed somehow to get most of it down. And immediately felt a little warmer, a little happier, as though lots and lots of very small creatures were hugging the tips of his fingers, his elbows, the backs of his knee, each and every toe.

'What was that?' he asked, when he was finally able to speak.

'Ah,' said Professor Yama, rubbing his hands together. 'A little concoction of my own making. I call it "Rescue Rememory".' He held up the little bottle, smiling broadly. 'Fast, effective relief from melancholia, heartsorrow and acute tristesse. Also, delicious.' He licked his fingers.

Jose got to his feet. The pounding in his head had completely gone and, though he remembered, vaguely, the sensation of blacking out, the images and sounds that had preceded it were already fading fast, like the memory of a bad dream.

'I do feel better,' he said. 'Much better. Thank you, Professor. Can I... may I go home now?'

Professor Yama's face grew grave and the starlight went out of his eyes. He looked at Jose with eyes so black they seemed to draw in the very air between them and swallow it up.

'No. I'm afraid not, Jose. Did Mishi not tell you? There is no going back. You are now a Gravepyres transitioner. And the only thing, the *only* thing for you to do – is to go on. Study hard, learn what you must, unlearn what you think you know. You must go on.'

With that, he raised his hand in a gesture of dismissal.

'Back to school, young man, and don't forget your bag. There is work to be done.'

The shouts and laughter of children playing rose up from the courtyard as Jose walked slowly along the gravel path from the dark cave entrance back towards the school. The sky was pearly grey and the air was still. In the courtyard, groups of transitioners were playing tag. It was like watching a flock of small, orange-feathered birds as they dodged around the ancient tree, their tunics flying. It must be break time, he supposed, and he ought to go and join in – but he didn't have the heart. How could they be *playing*? Didn't they have families? Didn't they want to go home?

The warm tingle of Professor Yama's medicine had fizzled away and a cold, empty dread filled his veins. He leaned against the wall, one knee bent and pressed against the stone, unable to shake off the Professor's words. *School for the recently deceased...?*

He slid down the wall and sat, his head in his hands, crushed by a wave of despair. Then his grandfather's voice came back to him. 'It's a mystery, Jose. The one thing in the whole universe that is one hundred per cent guaranteed to happen to happen to everyone, is the only thing that everyone thinks will never happen to *them*!' Ajja had thrown back his head and laughed – as though this was the most absurd and funniest joke he'd ever heard. Jose remembered thinking at the time that it was an odd thing to say. After all, Ajja was *old* – sixty at least – surely *he* knew he was going to die? But it was different for Jose: he was just a kid, not long into double-figures and, as far as he was concerned, life was one endless, glorious field that stretched away on all sides to the horizon and beyond. But then...

One of the small figures detached itself from the group and hop-skipped over to him. Jose looked up and found himself staring into Mishi's bright, mischievous eyes.

'Whatyoo doing?' she said.

'Nothing,' said Jose.

'Can I, too?' she said.

Jose shrugged. She squatted down next to him, small brown knees poking out of her tunic. She rested her chin on her hands, as he was doing, and assumed a similarly tragic expression. The two of them stared gloomily at the playing children.

'Are we done doing nothing?' she said, after a while.

'I suppose,' replied Jose.

Mishi continued doing nothing for a few seconds, but then decided that was enough. She jumped to her feet. 'Finished! What have you got next?'

She fished in his bag and drew out a sheet of paper. She unfolded it and scanned down a timetable. 'Cloudforming! I'm in Cloudforming too. We can go together. Do you know where to go? I think I do. I'm not sure. It's up there somewhere,' and she waved a hand up to one of the tall square towers. 'Are you new? I'm Mishi.'

Jose got up slowly.

'Yes, I know. We sat together yesterday, remember? Jose?'

Mishi looked at him with narrowed eyes. 'Y...es,' she said. 'I know *that*, obviously.'

Just then the gong rang out across the yard and the flock broke up into smaller groups as the transitioners began to file back into the building, off to their next lessons.

Mishi thrust Jose's timetable in front of his nose, and then did a little excited jump up and down on the spot. 'Chalo, chalo, Misssssster Joooaaaaazzzz, let's go. Last one there's a pig!' And with that, she dashed off, leaving Jose to follow in her wake.

He dragged his feet across the courtyard and into the main building. Mishi was nowhere to be seen. He

walked along a corridor, and then another, and up
a flight of stairs, his bag bumping against the back
of his legs. Left or right? Why aren't there any signs
in this wretched place, he thought, irritated, as he
made his way along another corridor which looked
exactly like the first two. By this time, judging by the
noises coming from behind the doors, lessons must
have begun. The corridors were empty. He turned the
corner and almost bumped into a boy with a round,
serious face and round, serious spectacles coming the
other way.

'Mind where you're going,' said the boy.

'Sorry,' said Jose.

The boy was about to head off when he stopped.
'Where *are* you going?'

'Er... the...er... Cloudforming?' stuttered Jose.

'Well, why are you going this way?' said the boy
with a frown. 'Are you new?'

Jose nodded sheepishly.

'That's okay – we all were once. Follow me.'

Jose trailed after him until they reached a doorway
with the word SKYLAB cut into the stone lintel across
the top.

'Well, here you are,' said the boy.

'Thanks,' said Jose. He noticed the boy was
wearing a badge on his tunic. 'Oh, you're a prefect,'
he said.

'Perfect, actually,' he replied, smoothing his neat
hair into place. He pointed to the badge, and sure

enough, now that Jose was looking at it closely, it *did* say 'Perfect', although the 'e' and the 'r' were jiggling a bit.

'Enjoy.' The boy held the door open for Jose and then headed back the way they had come.

The Skylab had two lines of tall workbenches running down the middle. Sticking out from the benches at intervals were metal pipes that ended in short lengths of flexible hose each fitted with a steel nozzle. They looked, to Jose, a bit like the hoses you use to wash your bottom in posh bathrooms. He spotted Mishi standing at one of the workstations, and chose an empty space on the bench behind her.

'Psst, Mishi,' he hissed.

She looked slightly startled – like she didn't recognise him at all – but then her face cleared. 'Jeff!' she said.

'Jose.'

'Jose!' she said. 'Where did you…'

Before she could finish her sentence, the door opened and everyone stood up as the teacher sailed in. She had a wide smile and a pleasantly freckly face beneath a fine frizz of sandy hair. Dressed in gauzy wraps and shawls, with a yellow scarf trailing from her shoulders, her outlines were slightly blurred – like sand whipped by the wind.

'Good mourning, children,' she trilled at them.

'Good mourning, Madame Cecilia,' they chorused back.

'Now zen, today we're going to do cumulus pileus with a few stratocumulus castellanus topped, for zosé zat can manage it, wiz a light coating of cirrus unicus.'

Great, thought Jose, fine. Why not?

Mishi reached into the drawer under the workbench and began pulling out a series of odd-looking implements, laying them out neatly in a line, like a dentist about to perform a root canal. Jose watched her surreptitiously and tried to copy what she was doing. She picked up one – a round hoop fixed to a long, thin wooden handle – and held it loosely in her left hand, while with her right she squeezed the nozzle and pulled it gently backwards, squirting out a fat streak of fluffy white stuff that floated a few inches above the worktop. She guided the steel hoop over and through it, waggling her hand now and then, and coaxed it into a series of bumps and ridges. Then, with another little wooden spike, she teased up the edges, poking and drawing out the white, plumping and shaping it until there floated... a perfect cloudscape. Jose was astonished at its beauty, and leaned closer to admire the thin, subtle streaks of vapour, as delicate as sheets of silk, overlaid with a towering mass of fluffy white, its edges burnished silver and its belly heavy with dark rain. As he watched, it began to move, pulsating gently and shifting softly between tones of light and shade: it was a mini-masterpiece.

Jose followed her actions exactly, and managed to create a sad white sausage.

Madame Cecilia swirled between the workbenches like a very slow, very gentle dust-storm. She stopped beside Jose and gave his cloud an experimental poke.

'More lift! *Allez-oop!*' she cried. 'Create! Let it fly!' And she floated off to examine the others'. Some had made cauliflowers, others flat pancakes. One looked like nothing more or less than – sorry, but it's true – a pile of white poop. None looked anything like an actual cloud except Mishi's, which was...

'*Merveilleux!*' cried Madame Cecelia ecstatically. '*C'est magnifique!*'

Jose and the others crowded around Mishi's workstation. 'How did you *do* that?' whispered Jose out of the corner of his mouth. Mishi smiled broadly. 'I'm a nat'ral,' she said, showing her large white teeth. 'Professor Styx said so.' She prodded Jose's blubbery cloud with one of her tools. 'Yours is a bit...' She wrinkled her nose, casting around for the exactly right word, '...rubbish, isn't it?'

When the lesson was over, the children put away their instruments, tidied their desks and scrumpled up the cloudstuff, dropping the wodges into the funnel next to the teacher's desk, ready to be reused by the next class. Mishi skipped away with the rest of the children, but Jose lingered at the end of the line. As he hastily destroyed his disastrous attempt and dropped it in the chute, Madame Cecelia looked up.

'Ah, Joseph, is it not?' she smiled at him. 'Is everysing all right?'

'Yes, thanks.' Jose hesitated for a moment. And then made up his mind. 'M...Madame Cecelia?' he stammered.

'*Oui.*'

'I think... I think there's been a mistake.'

She raised her eyebrows and waited for him to continue.

'I'm not actually supposed to be here. I... well, I already have a school: Bluebells International. In Delhi? The thing is...well, I have to get back. I'm supposed to give in my science project, and my mum and dad...they'll be...'

Madame Cecelia was looking at him with a strange expression on her face.

'You are a little 'omesick, *non*?' she said. 'It is eurly days, *mon petit*. It will take time but you will get used to sings here. You will get better. And before you know it, you'll feel right at 'ome.' She patted his hand.

Jose looked at his feet.

Home.

The thing was, he knew exactly what that was. It was waking up to the sound of crows outside his bedroom window and the smell of toast. It was hearing the lilting cry of the kabadi walla come to collect papers on his handcart on a Sunday morning.

It was playing cricket in the colony park with Aakash and Tanmai and Vaibhav. It was the feel of Pushkin's soft fur under his hand. It was the chopping sound of the fan when you lay on the bed with Ma on one side and Papa on the other after a big lunch in the heat of the afternoon and dozed off. It was the tchik-tchak of the bathroom light switch going on. It was new clothes at Diwali and presents on Christmas morning and buying spicy-sour bhel puri in leaf plates from the street stall on the corner when school was over. It was the smell of his mother's talcum powder and the feel of his sister's black hair that hadn't yet lost its baby fineness, and the scratch of his father's stubbly beard that certainly had. If this is what it's like to feel homesick, thought Jose, I'm not sure I want to get 'better' at all.

A fter the day's lessons were over, and the pearl-light of 'glimmer', as he was learning to call it, had given way to the ashy dark of 'gloom', Jose followed Mishi out of the study hall.

'Stupid calling it homework,' Jose was saying. 'They should just call everything "work". That's all it is anyway. Workworkwork.'

'I like it,' said Mishi. 'Don't you?'

Jose stopped walking for a moment to stare at her incredulously.

'Why? It doesn't make any sense. What's the point of it all?'

She pressed her lips together and nodded seriously.

'I suppose you're right. I hadn't thought of that. It *is* pointless.'

She composed her face to match the glumness on Jose's.

'We don't even stop for lunch.'

'Oh,' said Mishi, as they resumed walking. And then, with a little frown, 'Are you hungry?'

'Well, no,' said Jose. He suddenly realised that nothing had passed his lips since he arrived. Not a drop of water, nor a bit of food. Nothing in one end and – the thought came to him – nothing out the other either.

Something else was bothering him.

'What about sleep? Do you sleep?'

'Yes. No. Not exactly. We do horizontalling when it's gloom. I forgot.' She gave a little half laugh. 'I'm not very good at memorising. I forgot yesterglimmer, you weren't there, were you? In the RIP room, I mean. I think they've put you next to me, 'cos we're both new.'

Sometimes it was best, Jose was beginning to realise, to just let Mishi prattle on and hope that some semblance of meaning would bubble up eventually.

'Anyway,' she carried on, 'you'll see now. It's nearly deadtime.'

She pointed to a large wall clock he hadn't noticed before. It was held in the teeth of two grinning dragons, one on either side, like dogs going for the same ball. The dragons' tails snaked down and merged into the coloured carvings on the columns on either side. The hands of the clock pointed to eight-thirty, but all around the edge, instead of numbers there was a continuous band made up of two words: 'here now, here now, here now', or maybe, thought Jose suddenly, it just said 'nowhere, nowhere, nowhere...'

The RIP or 'rest-in-peace room', to give it its full title, was underneath the main building. Mishi followed a stream of transitioners as they trooped down a twisting stairwell, emerging at the bottom into a low-ceilinged dungeon-like room. There were rows upon rows of low wooden pallets, like raised beds in an allotment. At the head of each was a gravestone marker.

'Look,' said Mishi, pointing. 'I told you you were next to me.'

His name was etched into the stone at the head of one of the empty beds, next to another that said 'MISHI'. Each bed had its own small nightstand and candle, and a white sheet neatly folded at the foot. Some of the children were sitting up in bed, reading.

At each corner of the beds there were slim bamboo poles linked by strings of square prayerflags. Some, Jose noticed, looked new – like freshly laundered handkerchiefs pegged out to dry on a washing line. Others were so worn and faded that their colours had been washed away, and they looked like thin scraps of gossamer. The flags had been strung from one pole to the next, haphazardly across the whole room, as though the children were bedding down under a canopy of spiderwebs.

Mishi showed Jose where to change, and he did, swapping his day clothes for a long, floaty nightshirt that hung down around his ankles. She had done the same and was sitting on her bed waiting for him, her small, bare feet dangling a few inches off the floor.

Strangely, even after the long day of lessons, Jose wasn't tired in the least, and so he continued to watch the other children. Each time a child lay down and closed their eyes, the candle at their bedside went out as surely as if it had been snuffed out by their eyelids. There was something disturbing about the sight of children, who one minute earlier had been chatting and moving about, or sitting and reading quietly, suddenly falling absolutely still as soon as they lay down. Not a twitch or a murmur came from any of them. Not a flicker of an eyelid or the gentle fall and rise of breathing: nothing.

Soon there were only two candles left flickering in the long, dark room as Jose and Mishi sat facing each other.

'Mishi,' started Jose, 'how long have you been here?'

'Oh, not long really. Just before you, I think.'

'What do you mean, you think? You must know.'

'I think... I *thiiiink*...' She screwed her face up in concentration, and then abruptly gave up. 'I...don't know.'

'But on your homework for date of death you

put "last week". That can't be right,' Jose pressed on. 'I mean, you know loads, and your Cloudforming's brilliant...'

'...thankew,' she interjected.

'...and at least you know your way around. I don't think I'll *ever* figure this place out.'

Mishi, who was picking busily at her toenails, didn't reply.

'How long do we have to stay here?'

Mishi frowned and then sat up straight. She started to count off on her fingers. 'Well, first you've got to pass your cycle tests, and there's continuous assessment, and special projects, and group assignments, and then practicals and orals and extended and intended essays and then, once you get past aaaall of that...' her eyes went very big and round, '...there's the Ex-am.'

'Exam? What exam?'

'No, the *Ex*-am. The Exit-amination. It's the final test.'

'So... what you're saying is that if I study really, really hard, and I pass the exam –'

'– *Ex*-am...'

'– the *Ex*-am – that's the only way I'm going to be able to leave?'

Mishi nodded seriously. 'Yes, but you have pass Advanced Mathamythics with like 95 per cent, and...'

'But if you pass...' he interrupted.

She snorted. 'You'll never pass.'

'Yes, but if you do,' he persisted, '*then* what happens?'

'Then,' she leaned across to him and her eyes looked into his so deeply he thought he would drown in their caramel depths, 'then…you *gradulate*.'

'Gradulate?'

'Yuss.'

'What's that?'

'You wouldn't understand.'

'Yes, I would.'

'No, you wouldn't.'

'Yes, I would!'

'No, you wouldn't… and anyway,' she went on smugly, 'I'm not supposed to tell.'

'Rubbish!' Jose was outraged. 'I bet you don't even know!'

'Do too,' huffed Mishi and with that, she swung herself around, stretched out her legs, crossed her arms over her chest like she was a small, neat package ready to be posted. Her eyes snapped shut, the candle by her bedside went out, and Jose was left alone, staring into the dark.

At some point, Jose must have lain down himself and closed his eyes, because the next thing he knew a silver bell was chiming and all around the room the children were throwing off their shrouds and getting ready.

Outside, it was still quite gloomy. Whoever was in charge of the dimmer switch hadn't yet turned up the sky, and the children trooped into the main hall in no more than half-light. They sat on the floor in cross-legged rows, and the teachers in their yellow attire sat on small, fat cushions along either side. Maroon-robed monks and nuns sat in a line at the front, facing them. When everyone was settled, Madam Morte got up and marched to the front. She took down a large silver hoop from a hook on the wall and held it aloft.

'We will start with the Golden Sutra,' she announced. 'The Chant Memorius.'

She struck the hoop once with a small hammer and a high silver note rippled outward, like a pebble thrown into water. The monks struck up a low, guttural chanting, and the children, at every different pitch, joined in. *Leozainabalixijanetpiotr | Aleksandrsianimanimaha | Thadeoalanishanjyoti.* The sound rose and fell – it might have been Sanskrit, Latin, Ancient Aramaic or a mix of all three as far as Jose was concerned, but he closed his eyes and hummed along as best he could. As the three-note dirge of the Golden Sutra floated out into the air, the gloom began to lift, and by the time the chanting finally came to a close with another single *ting* of the silver hoop bell, it was full glimmer outside.

'From herenow on,' Madam Morte announced

in a clear, loud voice, 'there will be a full session of mnemonic chanting every other day – until further notice.' Ignoring groans from some of the children, she clapped her hands once. 'Off you go.'

As the transitioners filed out of the hall, Jose overheard Dr Chiplunker deep in conversation with Professor Styx. He caught the words 'lake' and 'crisis point', and saw Professor Styx shaking his head and saying in low tones, '…at its lowest ever, and no signs of…'

Then the Professor caught his eye and straightened up.

'Ah, Jose, good to see you up and about. We were worried about you. All better?'

'Yes, sir,' said Jose.

'Good, good. Now, do you know where your next class is? Entropology, I believe. Room 201.'

'Yes, sir,' said Jose, who had read his timetable but was still none the wiser. 'Entropy' he had heard of, maybe, but 'entropology'?

By the end of the double period, he was not just none the wiser, he actually felt quite a bit stupider. His head felt so stuffed with formulae and equations, there was really no room for anything else. Thermodynamics, the half-life of isotopes, closed systems and chaos theory – he didn't know about theory, but the jumble of terms bouncing around his skull certainly felt like chaos.

Thankfully, straight afterwards there was a short break period, and he and the rest of the class were let loose in the courtyard. While other kids hung around in groups, chatting or playing, some kicking a large black and red football around, Jose wandered towards the main gate. Every time he'd passed it before, it had been shut, with a heavy iron bar across it, but today, for some reason, the huge wooden door stood ever so slightly ajar. He looked around. There were no teachers about, and the kids seemed to be preoccupied with their own games.

Acting very casual, he eased himself through the gap and out the other side. He had no clear plan, just the sudden thought that if he had come *in* this way – that first day with Mishi – then surely it stood to reason that that was how he could get *out*. He glanced over his shoulder and then quickly ran down the steps that led to a small, flat ledge covered with small stones and gravel. He made his way to the edge and stopped. The ground fell away in front of him in a vertiginous cliff. There was no way down – no steps, no pathway. Jose lay on his belly and peered over the edge. He was on an overhang of rock, and behind him, the whole edifice of Gravepyres seemed to teeter on the edge. Looking down, he saw the rocky slope disappearing in a swirl of cloud far, far below. Suddenly nauseous, Jose got to his knees and crawled carefully backwards towards the heavy wooden gates. He got to his feet shakily and inched through the gap. Leaning back to push the door shut behind him, he rested for a moment against the reassuringly solid wood and gratefully closed his eyes.

'*M*ister Srinivas!'

A steely voice rang out across the yard.

He looked up to see Madame Morte bearing down on him.

Uh-oh, thought Jose, *now I'm in for it.*

She looked at him sternly. 'What *are* you doing lolling about here?' she said, but before he could even begin to reply, she carried on, 'We've been looking for you everywhere. You're on vulture duty today.'

Jose looked at her blankly.

'Oh, don't worry, they're perfectly harmless,' Madame Morte continued. 'Well, mostly harmless.'

She hurried Jose across the courtyard, shooing him ahead of her like a wayward chicken. Just then, she spotted a figure skipping along on the other side.

'Mishi! Mishi!' She beckoned the girl over. 'Be a dear and help Jose to get the vultures fed, would you? They must be getting awfully peckish by now.'

'Yes, Madame Morte,' said Mishi brightly.

'You'll need to go to the store first,' said Madame Morte. 'And do be sure to get the right food this time, dear. Apples it was last time, Jose, just imagine! Thought I'd never hear the end of it...'

Madame Morte hurried away. Mishi led Jose out of the main courtyard, down some steps and around to the back of the school. A cluster of small buildings lay higgledy-piggledy at the bottom of the slope – outhouses, farm buildings, storage rooms. They walked up to one that looked somewhere between a shop and a stable, with one of those split wooden doors that lets you swing open the top half. A sign was nailed up outside, painted in white letters on a dark blue rectangle of tin.

Houri McClury's Supply Stores
Purveyors of Finest Grosseries since Time Immemorial

And then in smaller letters below: No polybags.

Outside the store, there were woven baskets full of mysterious items, while bunches of what looked like dried herbs, onions and rather manky furry things dangled from the eaves.

Standing on tiptoe, Mishi peered over the lower half of the door into the dark interior. 'Hellooooo?' she called.

From inside came a voice, as sweet and musical as a silver bell: 'Mourning, mourning. I'll be with you in half a tick.'

A figure emerged from the shadows, and Jose looked up to see the most beautiful lady he had ever set eyes on. Her skin was so pearly white that it actually radiated light, and her wide-set, leaf-shaped eyes shone as brown as chestnuts beneath the sweeping wings of her eyebrows. She had a dainty nose, a small chin and lips the colour of tea-rose petals. Jose gazed up at her heart-shaped face and fell utterly and hopelessly in love.

'Och, it's you, Mishi,' said the vision, with a radiant smile, 'and who's your wee friend?' Which Jose thought was a little unfair, considering he was at least a head taller than Mishi.

'Oh,' said Mishi with a shrug, 'this is Jim. He's new. I'm looking after him.'

'Jose,' said Jose. 'My name's Jose. Rhymes with, er, rose.'

Houri McClury turned her luminous eyes on him. 'And a Jose by any *other* name would smell as sweet, I'm sure!' she said, with a tinkling laugh. 'I'm delighted to meet you, darling. Now then, Mishi, what'll you be wanting today? I've some lovely bacteria just come in, and a nice assortment of parasites.' She held up half a tick between her finger and thumb for them to see. 'Och, and a fresh delivery of slugs.'

'Thank you, but we just need a... um, some...' Mishi started, and then looked around a little vaguely. 'Ooooh, what are *those*?' She peered into a large glass jar of slimy things on the counter. 'Squirmy, wormy, shwerrrmy...' she cooed.

'...food,' said Jose quickly, 'Madame Morte asked us to get food for the vultures.'

'That's it,' said Mishi, straightening up. 'We're feeding them today.'

She followed Houri McClury into the back of the shop, leaving Jose to look around. There were buckets of squelchy things, baskets of leaf-mould, and jars of white powder labelled 'Mixed Spores' as well as a large wooden cask that was oozing a bit and had the word *Molluscs* painted on the side. On the shelves stood cans of Putrifaction and tubes of Ectoplasm. Then he noticed a deep stone tank of water. He bent over the dark surface – and jumped back with a start, narrowly avoiding some snapping claws. 'Mind the crustaceans,' came Houri McClury's voice from the back, where she was shovelling some entrails into a tin bucket. 'There we are, Mishi. I think that'll do it, don't you?'

Mishi nodded. She took one handle and Jose took the other, and together they heaved the bucket out of the shop. As they set off down the path, Jose looked back and stammered a quick 'Th... thank you, ma'am' over his shoulder. Standing in the doorway, Houri McClury gave him a smile that would have made his heart skip a beat – if only it had one to skip. Then she pointed in the opposite direction. 'That way, Mishi. Up to the Eerie, sweetheart.'

Mishi wheeled around as though she'd known that all along but just fancied a little diversion. They passed Houri McClury again and she nodded at them. 'Mind how you go,' she said as she waved them goodbye.

They rounded the corner and started up the hill behind the school, the bucket swinging between them. Mishi sang to herself: *Joaznjill wennup the hill to fetcha paila worta...*

As they were walking along, a thought came to Jose.

'Mishi, you know you were saying the other day about vultures...'

'Mmm?'

'You said I couldn't go home, not unless I was a vulture. Do you mean that vultures can go back to the real world?'

'You mean the Land of the Living? Well, yes,' she shrugged. 'Everyone knows *that*.'

'But – I mean, how?'

'Through the lake, of course.'

'What lake?'

'The *laaaaake*,' she said, spreading her hands and rolling her eyes like *he* was the idiot.

'I heard Professor Styx saying something about a lake this morning. You mean that lake?'

Mishi plonked her side of the bucket down and Jose quickly did the same to avoid some gory spillage.

'There is only one lake. Want to see?' she said.

Jose nodded.

Leaving the bucket on the path, Mishi led the way along a smaller lane that forked off to the left, through a hillside dotted with pine trees, and up a small rise. Slipping a little on the soft brown needles carpeting the floor, Jose scrambled up behind her, and they emerged at the edge of a steep-sided valley, at the bottom of which lay a shining pool of silver water, rimmed on all sides by a wide strip of cracked earth and mud.

'Lake Lachrymosa,' Mishi said softly.

The water lay like a dish of mercury, shining much more brightly than the dull sky above. The clouds looked down at their reflections, which the lake polished and returned with extra radiance. Sky and water, water and sky, gazing at each other, unable to look away.

'It's beautiful,' said Jose in a whisper. 'Can we get down there?'

Mishi pointed to a winding footpath that led around the edge and towards a narrow wooden jetty that jutted out into the water.

'That path leads back to the school, to the back of the grosserie store, near the monks' quarters,' she said.

Jose looked across to the far side, where the hills rose and undulated, vanishing in a blue-grey haze in the distance.

'And what's over there?' he asked.

'Myst,' said Mishi.

'Mist?'

'Myst,' she said emphatically. 'With a "y".'

Jose thought it was a bit rich of Mishi to correct anyone else's spelling.

'Okay, but I mean, what's beyond that?'

'Mountains, I think,' said Mishi. 'Nobody knows really. Might just be more myst. Might be it's a mystery,' she giggled. Then she slapped her forehead. 'Yikes. Vultures.'

They hurried back down the slope, retrieved the bucket and carried on walking along the path. After a while, Mishi stopped to gaze up at another, much larger hill, at the top of which stood a tall, ruined-looking tower, pointing accusingly up at the clouds.

'Look,' she said, putting the bucket down, 'here they come.'

Dark shadows were emerging from the top of the tower, launching themselves one by one from the highest point like ash blown from the smouldering tip of an incense stick, floating on huge outspread wings, and circling the air with wingtips splayed and curled upward like temple dancers' fingers.

'Quick,' said Mishi, grabbing the bucket. Jose took the other handle and together they tipped the gory contents on to the grass and took a few paces back. The vultures wheeled overhead like a flock of pterodactyls, growing bigger as they circled closer with each tilt of their wings, each silent beat in the still air, their heads casting this way and that. They were now so close that Jose could see the beady flash of their white-rimmed eyes. They dropped down, claws outstretched, and ran-hopped clumsily towards the pile of bloody gloop and gristle, folding their wings behind them, their naked necks outstretched.

Within minutes of the first vulture landing, the ground had vanished beneath a scrum of feathers and claws. Occasionally a long bald neck would snake up, pulling a skein of flesh with its viciously hooked beak, its head daubed in a war-paint of blood, only to disappear again into the squawking, writhing pile of black, brown and white feathers.

One particularly large, white-bellied vulture with a pinkish ruff at the base of its crooked neck, landed near them with two powerful backbeats of its wings. Ignoring the scrum, it hopped over to the kids and craned its scrawny neck to examine the bucket which lay on its side nearby.

'No apples today then, young lady?' said the vulture, scrutinising Mishi with one glinting yellow eye. It waved its massive hooked beak over the gory slop that smeared the grass red. 'Mmmm, smells *divine*,' the vulture declared. Then it cocked its head to one side. 'But – where are my manners? Mishi dear, aren't you going to introduce me to your new friend?'

'This is J... Jose,' said Mishi. It finally seemed to be sinking in, thought Jose, relieved.

'Myself, Perveen Pestonji Peckerwala, at your service,' said the vulture, and dipped her head towards Jose in a gracious bow.

'Pleased to meet you,' replied Jose, bowing in turn and feeling slightly overawed. He noticed there were some bits left in the bottom of the bucket. 'Have some, er, liver?'

The vulture took a step closer. The feathers of her ruff stood out as Perveen dropped her head down for a closer look. 'Well, I really shouldn't. It goes straight to my thighs. Perhaps just a nibble...'

Jose watched, fascinated and slightly queasy, as she hoiked a dripping lump of meat from the bottom of the bucket, threw back her head and gobbled it up.

Suddenly, a large shadow fell over them. Jose looked up to see an enormous dark shape sailing low overhead. The vultures scattered backwards, hopping like ungainly turkeys, their wings held out stiffly, leaving an empty circle of bone-strewn, blood-stained grass in the centre of which lay a large, ghastly heart.

Jose's hair riffled with the throb of powerful wings as a huge bird landed in the clearing and stalked forward, its wings angled forward and half-spread like a cloak, its head low as though it protruded from the middle of its chest. Jose nervously eyed the wicked-looking beak – as long as his forearm, a blueish band above the black tip – as the vulture tore into the meat, and Madame Morte's less-than-reassuring words came back to him: 'Mostly harmless anyway.'

'Our leader,' whispered Perveen to Jose out of the side of her beak. 'His Excellency, El Condor Pasa.'

'Wow,' said Jose. 'He's big.'

Jose felt the cold touch of Mishi's hand on his. 'Come on,' she said, tugging him away, 'we'd better get back.'

VII

The rest of the day was spent like the one before, trooping from lesson to lesson, with one or two breaks from glimmer to gloom, then painful amounts of 'home' work until they could finally head down to the RIP room to horizontal.

Mishi trotted beside him from one class to the next, jabbering away incessantly. Occasionally what she said made sense, but usually she seemed off on what Jose thought of by now as Planet Mishi. She still kept forgetting his name, but that didn't really seem to bother her. She took great pleasure in pointing out all the different parts of the school: the stationery store, where the books and papers were kept; the Staff Room, where the teachers kept their staffs; the Skullery where they kept their... well, I'm sure you can guess. '...and in there, that's the library,' she said, pointing.

'Yes, you said that before,' said Jose. And then he stopped.

'Can you borrow books?' he asked.

Mishi rolled her eyes. 'It's a *library*, duh!'

'What I mean is, can I go in and borrow a book for later? I like to read before I go to…I mean, when I horizontal.'

'Okay,' said Mishi and heaved open the library door.

With its tall, arched wooden struts that met high overhead, the library resembled a huge upturned ship. There were racks upon racks of books on several levels, each stacked on top of the other on increasingly narrow balconies and accessed on extendable, wheeled ladders. In one corner several monks and nuns were carefully illuminating a sheaf of palm manuscripts, and in the centre of the library was a circular counter at which a young nun was reading, chin on one hand. As they approached, she put a bookmark in her paperback and carefully placed it on the counter.

'Excuse me,' said Jose, 'but have you got anything on vultures?'

'And I want a nice book with lots of pictures, please,' added Mishi.

The nun rose wordlessly and pointed Jose to a rack opposite the counter. Then she took Mishi by the hand and led her to the children's section which was full of large, slim, colourful books and had brightly embroidered cushions scattered on the floor. Mishi was soon happily immersed in a book about a little fairy called Tinkytonk and her adventures in Acornland.

Jose scanned the shelf in front of him. *Making Heavy Weather: A Life in Cloudmaking* by Geoffrey Herringbone. *Transubstantiation: The Subtle Art* by Qasim Al-Umani. *A Brief History of Timelessness* volumes I–XX by Cristabel J. Dorkin. They all looked pretty dull. Then he noticed a large tome bound in dark red leather on which the title was embossed in curling letters of gold: *The Wind Beneath their Wings: The Way of the Vulture* by Miguel Xavier Perera.

He took the book from the shelf and found a quiet corner. He opened it at random, balancing it on his knees, and began to read.

Unlike most other birds, Turkey vultures have an acute sense of smell.

Well, that certainly checked out, the way Perveen and co. had swooped down from the Eerie.

Many people assume – wrongly – that vultures are birds of prey. This is erroneous, given that vultures feed only on the carcasses of already dead animals.

Jose found himself thinking about the vulture chief and his huge, curved beak, and wondered how the vultures in the Land of the Dead viewed small transitioners. El Condor Pasa looked like he could devour an entire classroom and not even burp. Jose gave an involuntary shiver and carried on reading.

> Indeed, when it comes to vultures, the very classification of 'prey' and 'predator' requires rethinking. Gentle creatures, they do not kill, but rather perform a vital function in the ecosystem, cleaning up and disposing of carcasses that can otherwise become a breeding ground for disease. Their stomachs contain high levels of acid that destroys anthrax, cholera and other bacteria that would be fatal for other creatures.

Jose flipped a few pages and stopped at a chapter called 'Vultures in Myth and Legend'.

> Recent genetic analyses reveal that the nearest relative of the Turkey Vulture, or Buzzard, is in fact, a bird more commonly associated with the delivery of babies, the Stork. To the Ancient Assyrians, the Vulture was Sunyata, a semi-divine entity symbolising the non-separated union between the day and night. Ancient Egyptians worshipped the Goddess Nephthys in the form of a Vulture and believed that all Vultures were female, and were

born not from an egg, but created from the air itself. In Greek mythology, the Vulture is a descendant of the Griffin, and was thought to symbolise the non-dual oneness of spirit and matter, good and evil, as both guardian and avenger, the only creature able to move between the realms of the living and the dead...

Bingo.

Mishi was right. So... if the vultures could fly to the Land of the Living, then it was possible. It was possible! He could get back. He could get to his parents, to his sister. He could let them know where he was, that he was alright. Not that he was... *Oh god,* he thought, *just to see them again. Just to see them – to let them know I'm alright.* More than anything he wanted to stop that sound, that unearthly sound, escaping his mother's lips. *I would do anything, anything to stop that. I just have to figure out how.*

Jose closed the book, got up and took it to the counter. The librarinun stamped the ticket in the front and handed it back to him, doing the same for Mishi. The children tucked their treasures under their arms and left.

'I like stories,' Mishi was saying as they headed back to the RIP room, 'but reading is really hard. Pictures are good. I like pictures. Sometimes, if I ask, Professor Styx reads me a deadtime story...' but Jose wasn't really listening. His mind was already far away.

Later, as the RIP room lay cold and dark, Jose stared up at the canopy of faded prayer flags above him, thoughts swirling around his head. He tossed and turned, feeling itchy and restless. 'I'm not supposed to be here,' he said quietly to himself.

It was no good. He felt claustrophobic lying there. So, as quietly as he could, he kicked off his shroud, got up, and tiptoed out of the room and up the spiral staircase to the entrance hall. The door hinged open with a squeaky groan, and he made his way across the courtyard, the flagstones cool and smooth beneath his bare feet. Through an archway he crept, and down past Houri McClury's supply shop, which stood dark and silent, the fringe of herbs hanging from the eaves like eyelashes on a sleeping face. Instead of following the path towards the Eerie, he veered left, past the dark huts where the monks and nuns stayed, under the low dark trees and out towards the lake.

The water lay glinting blackly beneath the deep, dark sky. He walked along the edge of the lake until he reached a rickety wooden jetty. He made his way to the very end and sat, his bare feet dangling just above the still, shining water. Looking down, Jose was suddenly overwhelmed with a terrible, aching sadness that he had been fighting off all day. He missed – well, he missed absolutely everything: his mother, his father, his sister, their house, his cat, his friends, his cricket bat, the sound of parakeets in the morning, the feel of the monsoon rain, the smell of onions frying, his special pencil box with the secret compartment, his bed, his rollerblades – just everything. A tear leaked out of one eye, rolled its way down the left side of his nose, and fell, plop, into the water.

Before the ripples had subsided, or the next tear had a chance to form, Jose felt a hand on his shoulder. 'Sadness,' said Professor Styx, 'in a place like this? A drop in the ocean, dear boy, a drop in the ocean.'

'I... I couldn't sl...horizontal,' said Jose.

'It's alright,' said the Professor kindly, settling down on the jetty next to him. 'I often come out here when it's dark. It's a good place to clear the mind.'

They sat there together for a while, one small boy and one tall, bony man, each lost in his own thoughts. After a while, Jose said hesitantly, 'Professor, I got this book from the library, and I was wondering if... if... I mean, is it true that the vultures can get through to the real wo... I mean the Land of the Living?'

'Yes,' Professor Styx nodded. 'That's right.'

'Through the lake?'

'Yes,' said Professor Styx, and then he hesitated and looked down with a frown. 'At least, they used to.'

'What do you mean?' said Jose.

Professor Styx looked out across the waters and then pointed. 'See over there?' he said. 'Where all those reeds and grasses are? All that mud? That should all be underwater. The lake is shrinking and nobody knows why.'

He fell silent for a moment.

'The river that feeds the lake no longer flows. Oh, we've tried everything to replenish the waters, but it seems hopeless. The only thing that helps a bit is the chanting – but even the Chant Memorius only seems to slow the rate of reduction. It doesn't stop it altogether – and nobody knows how to reverse it. Not even Professorr Yama,' he said, with something like despair in his voice. He shook his head sadly. 'The vultures are finding it harder and harder to get through. Lake Lachrymosa is dying, Jose, and there's not a thing we can do about it.'

VIII

The next day, as Jose sat in Dr Chiplunker's class (they were Seeing a paperclip – thrilling), Professor Styx's words kept coming back to him. He hadn't said that the vultures *couldn't* get through the lake, only that it was getting 'harder and harder'. Surely, if the vultures could do it, then so could he? He was a pretty good swimmer, and he wouldn't even have to hold his breath – because he didn't have any breath to hold. Maybe he could slip out again when everyone was horizontalling and dive into the lake. He shuddered a bit at the thought of slipping into that black water. He wondered if you could drown if you were already dead...

'*Srinivas!*' Thwack! Dr Chiplunker's ruler slammed down on the desk. 'Are you, or are you not, PRESENT?'

Jose retrieved his paperclip from the floor.

By gloom, he had made up his mind.

While the other transitioners were busy in the study hall doing homework, Jose sneaked out of the school again. This time he avoided the lake and trudged up the hill alone, in the dim half-dark. Tiny bones crunched beneath his feet as he approached the base of the Eerie. He was standing looking up at the great stone tower, searching for a way to get in, when he noticed a large brass bell hanging from a chain. It looked just like the bells that used to hang in their local temple in Delhi. When he was little, his father used to lift him onto his shoulders so he could reach the heavy clapper.

Gathering all his strength, he took a running jump at it and managed to just brush the clapper with the tips of his fingers. It swung once, and a deep clang rang out into the still air.

He stepped backwards and felt a rush of cool wind on his face as a shadow swooped down out of the dark sky.

'Why, hello fledgling,' said Perveen Peckerwala, landing beside him. 'What are you doing back here?'

'I need to...' Jose began, and then stopped. He didn't want to appear rude. 'That is, I wondered if I could maybe speak to El Condor Pasa?'

Perveen ruffled her feathers and drew herself up to her considerable height. 'His Excellency is sleeping,' she replied grandly. 'He cannot be disturbed.'

'Perveen,' a deep voice intoned, startling both of them, 'El Condor eez never disturbed.'

The huge vulture had arrived, silent as nightfall, and stood behind them.

'I know jou,' he said, eyeing Jose.

'You do?' said Jose, nervously.

'Jes,' said El Condor. 'Jou breeng us da deleeeecious meat. Not da terrible fruits like Mishi – yeauch. Wassa problem, keed? Jou want to speak with El Condor?'

Now he was actually standing in front of him, all the things Jose had planned to say to El Condor seemed stupid, inadequate, ridiculous. The bird stood taller than Jose himself, his magnificent wings folded, the dark bars on his flight feathers displayed like military stripes. His legs were covered in overlapping grey scales, each splayed foot was the size of a paving slab and ended with four deadly-looking black talons. His beak was a matching black at the tip, but had a lighter band above it, like a rim of blue steel, and his eyes were a series of concentric rings: a bright red outer rim, thin black inner, a white iris and a piercing black pupil bang in the centre. The look he fixed on Jose pierced him to the very bones. El Condor seemed to be weighing up the options: tear into him straight away or save him for dessert.

'Wassa matter?' said the vulture. 'Lost your tongue, ay?'

Jose gulped. 'I... I got a book... from the library,' he stammered. 'It said that vultures – that you – can travel between the world of the living and the dead.' Perveen and El Condor exchanged a meaningful look. Jose bravely carried on. 'And I thought... that... maybe... if you could, then maybe I could too... you know, come along with you... on your... back. Or something,' he ended lamely.

El Condor burst out laughing. If you've ever heard a vulture laugh, you'll know exactly what that sounded like. And if you haven't, well, just imagine a goose playing a trombone while being strangled to death by an anaconda.

Perveen raised a huge hooked claw and scratched the corner of her eye.

'The thing is, Jose dear, you can't go back. You're... well,' she paused delicately, 'you're deceased. Not to put too fine a point on it, you're – um, *dead*. You're also... human,' she said with a mixture of what to Jose's ears sounded like both pity and scorn. 'You see, only we vultures can pass unharmed through the waters of the Sacred Lake. It has been so since time began, and the realms of the Living and the Dead came into being, created by a single feather from the breast of the Great Gryphon Herself...' She fluffed up her ruff and her gimlet eye shone with pride. 'But humans...'

'I know you can't help it,' she went on. 'You

can't choose your species, I always say. But you must have seen what's happening on the Other Side? It's becoming intolerable, really it is. Eggs with such thin little shells. Chicks,' her voice cracked with emotion, 'little chicks dying before they're born. Nowhere to nest, nowhere to fly, and the sickness! The terrible sickness. At least we're safe here.' She sighed extravagantly and wiped away a tear with her wingtip. 'Honestly, Jose dear, are you sure you even *want* to go back?'

'Humans, pah! Miserable stumpytoed plodders. Trashdumpers!' El Condor harrumphed in the background, ruffling his feathers and stomping his talons. 'No-brain, meat-poisoning, concrete-loving uglifiers.'

'Yes. Quite,' said Perveen, mollifying El Condor with a look.

'Perveen's right, keed,' said El Condor. 'Dis place?' He swept a wide wing over the still, grey land. 'It's not so bad.'

Jose knew all about it. The noise pollution, the air pollution, climate change, ecosystems, greenhouse gases, poisoned rivers, plastic seas – he'd lost count of the number of 'Think Green, Go Green' posters they'd been forced to make at school. But all he could think about was how much he missed the bustle and the crowds; he would trade the most beautiful music in the whole world for the tumultuous, chaotic roar of Delhi traffic. He would give his right arm for a single lungful of its stinking, fume-laden air. He had to make them see, he had to make them understand: it was his *home*.

'I have to get back,' he said, a note of quiet desperation creeping into his voice. 'My mum and dad need me. I have to let them know that I'm alright. Even if I'm not,' he sniffed, 'not really. Your Excellency, what if...,' Jose went on, thinking on his feet, 'I mean, even if *I* can't go back, would you at least be able to take them a message?'

El Condor narrowed his eyes. 'Lemme get this straight, keed,' he said advancing on Jose. 'Jou – little bitty no-wings – want me, El Condor Pasa, Supreme Commander of Gyps Himalayenthis, Tenuirostris, Indicus, Fulvus and Bengalensis, Lord of the High Thermals, Conquistador of the Raging Storm, The Golden Purifier...'

'... Guardian of the Sacred Updraft...' Perveen chipped in.

'Jes, jes, Guardian of the... anyway, jou want *me* to deliver a *message* to jour mami-papi for *jou?*'

'Er... yes,' said Jose. 'Please,' he added politely.

Perveen interceded before El Condor could explode again, and ushered him to one side with her wing. They stood together in a huddle, muttering. Finally, El Condor stretched his long snake-like neck and then folded it into himself. Wings angled forward on either side and head lowered, the huge bird stalked back until his beak was a few inches from Jose's nose.

'Hokay, keed,' he said, with quiet menace. 'Suppose – chuss suppose – hypotheckitally, I could take a message to da mami-papi little human-peeps. What would jou say, ay?'

Jose thought hard.

'Tell them, um, that I love them.'

El Condor's eyes widened and he let out a squawk of raucous laughter. Then he choked and had to be repeatedly thumped on the back by Perveen. With tears in his eyes, he finally croaked, 'Jou too much, keed. "I luff them"! Of course you luff them, stoopid. Thees is not a birthday card, hokay? You gotta come up wid somethin' bedder dan dat.' He turned to leave.

'Okay, okay,' said Jose hurriedly. 'Tell them, I mi...'

'Pleeeeeease, don' tell me that you mees them! Perveen, chiquita, where d'jou find dis dodo?'

Jose stood downcast. There were tears in his eyes too, but they weren't tears of laughter. El Condor glanced at him and fell silent.

'Leesten. Anyways, it ain't gonna happen.' El Condor gave an eloquent shrug of his great, feathered shoulders, 'Not with da lake like it is.'

'Look at it,' said Perveen, pointing one wingtip to the lakeshore. She shook her head sadly. 'No one's come through for months. We don't even know if there is anyone left on the other side.'

'Ay, chiquita.' El Condor drew her under one enormous wing. 'Don' say that. We'll figure it out, eh?'

'I'm sorry, Jose, but that's just how it is,' Perveen said in a broken voice. 'You'd better get back to school. I'm sorry we can't help.' She hunkered down on her great legs and then ran down the slope, swooping off in a graceful glide.

'She's right,' said El Condor, 'she always is. So long, keed.' With a rueful shake of his tail feathers, he launched himself after Perveen into the silent air.

IX

Jose expected everyone to be horizontalling by the time he got back, but the windows of the study hall flickered with light and inside, the other kids were still hunched over their worksheets, scribbling away. Jose slipped onto the bench next to Mishi.

'Where've you been?' she whispered.

'Never mind,' he said, and took out his notebooks. Scare Studies, Mathamythics – none of that mattered any more. The only thing that mattered was getting back to his family. Even if the vultures wouldn't help him, there had to had to *had to* be a way. 'Think it through,' his mother always used to say when he was stuck on a problem, 'and when you can't think through it, think around it.' Jose refused to accept that he was stuck here forever, that he would never see his family again. He bit the side of his thumb and frowned with furious concentration. The answer had to be out there... he just had to figure it out.

From then on, Jose spent every break time in the library, searching and searching – he wasn't sure what for – a clue, or an idea, or inspiration. He consulted books on philosophy, philology, anthropology and zoology; astrophysics and biochemistry; geometry and trigonometry. He skimmed through books of stories: myths and legends; folklore and fairy tales. He scanned pictures and pored over maps. He even spent some time in the gardening and cookery section. He went most often to the section marked 'Self-help' because, he reasoned, help was what his self needed most, but apart from learning that there were (apparently) seven steps to becoming an effective leader, he came away empty-handed.

Then, one glimmer, just as he was about to give up, the librarinun wandered over. 'You might like this,' she said. 'Careful. It's very old.'

She placed a large leather-bound book on the desk in front of him. He brushed the dust off the cover and read the title: *Leechdoms, Wortcunning and Starcraft: An Illustrated Herbarium.*

The spine creaked and cracked a bit as he opened it up. How the librarinun thought this was going to help him was beyond Jose, but he dutifully started to turn the pages. On the title page, in swirly letters, there was a dedication: 'To thofe who feek.' Once he realised that the book was written in that old-fashioned script where all the 's's look like 'f's, the writing – with its illuminated letters and curious illustrations – began to make sense. The paintings inside were of plants the like of which he had never seen. A lily with a tiger's mouth full of teeth, a plant with leaves like clover and roots shaped like little people with grinning faces and tapering fingers, another which sprouted eyes instead of petals. Then Jose came to a page which showed a painting of a life-size hand. In the palm of the hand was a small white circle from which flares of white light radiated outwards, spilling off the edge of the page. Under the painting were three simple words: *Feed of hope.*

A feed of ...? No – a *seed* of hope? Jose stared at the painting, his eyes wide.

Could this be the answer? What would it do, this seed? What was it for?

Jose turned the page, but unlike the other plants that had explanations of what they were used for, there was nothing more about the seed of hope. No clue as to where it grew or what it grew on. He scanned the rest of the book and looked through the index – but that was it. One page, one illustration, and three words.

But what words. If there was one thing that Jose needed right now, it was hope. A slender thread of possibility that he played with in his mind, twisting and turning it into a rope, strong enough to bear the weight of his longing... *With a seed of hope, I might get through the lake*, he thought to himself. He imagined dropping it like a pearl into the black waters, and the waters receding, opening up a hole through which he could fall – diving out of this dead Hell and back to the Land of the Living, back to the world that he knew, that wonderful world of breathing people with beating hearts and blood in their veins. Jose shut the book and clutched it to his chest. He shook his head, remembering Perveen's words. He didn't care if he was 'only Human'. It wasn't hopeless, and he wasn't going to give up.

Jose thanked the librarinun as he gave the book back. She took it with a faraway half-smile, and watched him as he hurried out.

If there was one person at Gravepyres who might be able to help him, Jose thought, it was Houri McClury. She seemed to know about plants and seeds and spores and stuff. Maybe she even *had* a seed of hope in all those jars and bottles in her store! He picked up the pace and fairly ran along the courtyard and out of the school.

He skidded to a halt outside the Grosserie and rattled the shutters. 'Hello?' he called out. 'Hello? Is anyone there?'

'Store's closed, dear,' came a silvery voice. 'Come back at glimmertime…'

'I don't need to buy anything,' said Jose, urgently. 'I need your help.'

He heard a latch scraping back, and the top half of the door swung outwards.

Houri McClury peered out, her face emerging from the darkness as radiantly as the moon appearing from behind clouds.

'Och it's you, Jose,' she said. 'Come in, come in.'

She swung open the door and ushered him inside, and then dragged up a wooden barrel for him to perch on. She settled down on another and sat facing him in the flickering candlelight.

'Now,' she said, 'what's all this about?'

He explained as best as he could about the Herbarium and the library. Houri McClury sat patiently and heard him out. '...And I wondered, if maybe you have a seed of hope in your supplies?' he ended.

'A seed of hope?' She laughed a tinkling silvery laugh. 'Now wouldn't *that* be something, eh?' Then, with her eyes still sparkling, she said, 'It's not a real seed, sweetheart. All those tales of galloping off to find the seed of hope at the Eternal Spring – they're just fairy stories and songs. Och now, how does it go...' And she began to sing in a low, dreamy voice.

A wine made from smiles
And a rainbow cake
A cup of sweet water
From yon salty lake
Time in your pocket

And love in your locket
And a seed for hope in your hand, in your hand,
A seed for hope in your hand.

As her voice rose, Jose's heart sank.

'But it was in the *Herbarium*,' he said when she finished. 'It was in a book – with illustrations and everything...'

Houri shifted on her seat. 'You cannae believe everything you read in books, Jose, you know that. I mean, may be it is real, but not *real*, d'you see? Like – I don't know, like love is real, or anger. You cannae pick it up, like a stone. But just because it's not real dusnae mean it's not true. What you need to do,' she said, leaning forward earnestly, 'is look...'

'What,' he burst out angrily, "look inside yourself"? Is that what you're going to say? That's no good! How is that supposed to help –' He just managed to stop himself from saying 'my mother' and left it at that.

Houri put her hands in her lap and looked at them.

'And the Eternal Spring,' Jose went on, 'I suppose that's not real either.'

'We...eell,' she said, 'no, no that's real enough. Where else d'you suppose the River of Time starts?'

'I...I...' began Jose. 'Hang on. There's an actual River of *Time*?'

'The river that runs into the lake, of course. Honestly, d'they teach you nothing at that school?'

Jose stood up. 'Thank you, Houri McClury ma'am. Thank you very much. And... um... you've got a very beautiful voice.'

She took his hands in her own and gave them a squeeze. 'Well,' she said, 'Thank you, laddie. You'd best be off.'

It wasn't much to go on – a fictitious seed that might be found, if it existed at all, at the source of a very mythical-sounding river, wherever on earth that might be – but it was all he had. The beginnings of some kind of plan were taking shape in his head, and he clutched at the straw like a drowning man and held on fast.

There's a saying in the Land of the Living: 'There's no time like the present.' Well, there's a saying in the Land of the Dead too: 'There's no time *but* the present', and once Jose had made up his mind, he wanted to set off at once.

To Jose, every day at Gravepyres seemed to last an eternity, but that day seemed twice as long as usual. The children went to their lessons: Mathamythics (nonsensical), Cloudforming (cirrocumulous stratiformis lacunousus or, in Jose's case, 'fat white sausage' – again), Seeing (they stared at a silhouette of two black faces on a white vase for an hour – he could still see them throbbing red and green when he shut his eyes), interspersed with break times.

After they had finished their mountains of homework, and the light had finally faded from the sky, the transitioners lay in the RIP room, safe beneath their shrouds. Eyes drooped shut, and one by one the candles went out until finally the room fell dark: not a footstep or a cough or a sigh could be heard. Jose blinked his candle out and lay there staring up at the ceiling until he could bear it no longer. Then he quietly got up, dressed, wrapped a shawl around his shoulders and tiptoed out, carrying his sandals.

He sat on the steps leading down to the silent courtyard to strap on his shoes. The grey flagstones glinted like gunmetal in the darkness; the stone dragonheads above the lintel stared down at him with unseeing eyes. He was about to stand up when a tap on his back almost made him jump out of his skin.

'Where you going?'

It was Mishi.

'Shhhhh,' Jose shushed her urgently. 'I'm...um... I'm just, er... nowhere.'

Mishi narrowed her eyes.

'You're spoze to be horizontalling,' she said accusingly.

'Yes, I know. I just...'

'I'm going to tell Madame Morte,' said Mishi, crossing her arms.

'No! No, you mustn't,' said Jose, panicking.

'Will too,' she said mutinously, 'unless you tell me where you're going RIGHT NOW!'

'Alright, alright,' said Jose, looking around nervously. 'Keep your hair on. Listen, I'm going to find the source of the river.'

'WHAT?!' Mishi looked horrified. 'But, but, you're not ALLOWED.'

'Yes, I sort of guessed that. That's why we've got to be *really quiet.*'

'It's against the Rules,' Mishi hissed at him. 'You'll get rusty-gated! You can't go.'

'You can't stop me,' said Jose (wondering to himself what getting rusty-gated meant. Whatever it was, it didn't sound good).

They glared at each other.

'Alright then,' said Mishi with an air of finality, 'I'm coming too.'

'What?? You can't!'

'Professor Styx told me to look after you. So there.'

'But... but...'

'And he also said to me, no buts,' said Mishi. 'And anyway,' she added, her eyes suddenly sparkling, 'it's a *quest*. I always wanted to do a quest. Tinkytonk and Cowbell have to go on a quest to find the magic acorn to beat the wicked wizard Puffalot. Like that.'

Jose looked at her for a minute. The courtyard was still silent. There wasn't a soul about. He was (secretly) rather nervous about going off all on his own, and (very secretly) rather liked the idea of having someone along with him. Even if that someone was a small, rather odd girl fixated on fairy tales and with the memory of a goldfish.

'Alright then,' he said finally. 'But we're going to need help.'

The two children crept out of the courtyard and made their way up the hill towards the Eerie. Jose clanged the bell and two dark familiar shapes floated down towards them.

'A little late for transitioners to be out, isn't it?' said Perveen, settling her wings.

'It's *important*,' said Mishi abruptly and stood there sturdily, her arms folded, a frown on her face.

'What's this about, keed?' rumbled El Condor.

Mishi looked at Jose and signalled with her eyes for him to explain. He cleared his throat.

'You said the lake was drying up, and you couldn't get through – right?' he began.

The vultures nodded.

'Well, suppose that you could. I mean, suppose that we found out what was wrong and fixed it?'

'Fix it? You?' El Condor looked down on them from his full height.

'Or... somebody could. At least we find out what's wrong. It has to be something upstream – you know, maybe blocking it, or diverting the water, or something. No one seems to know why this is happening, but it has to be something like that. If you could help to get us upriver we could find out...'

'Jose,' Perveen interrupted, 'do you think we haven't tried? You don't understand,' she went on, and gestured for them to follow her. She hopped to the top of a small rise behind the tower and spread out her wing, pointing across the lake to the dark horizon. 'The river flows down from the mountains – the land beyond the myst,' she said. 'We can't go beyond that.'

'It's a no-fly zone,' intoned El Condor.

'What, even for you?' asked Jose.

El Condor looked a little miffed, but ruffled his feathers and nodded. 'Even for me,' he conceded. 'Vultures cannot fly into Kozitsthereistan...'

'Kozitswhatiswho?' said Jose.

'Kozitsthereistan,' he repeated. El Condor narrowed his eyes and looked away into the distance. 'Ain't nobody goes there, my friend. And if they do – ain't nobody comes back.' He let that sink in, and then turned to leave. 'Hokay, tha's it? Come, Perveen. Let's go.'

Jose bit his lip and stood his ground.

'Then that's where we're going,' he said, sounding a lot braver than he felt. He carried on, the words tumbling out as he threw caution to the wind. 'It's okay if you won't help us, it doesn't matter. If you want to just sit there and let the lake dry up *completely* and do nothing, that's fine. No vultures going to the Land of the Living, and *none* able to get through to here – because, because that's what it means, doesn't it? That's what's going to happen. We don't need your help: we're going anyway. Just point us in the right direction. We'll make it on our own.'

'That's right,' said Mishi. She stood next to Jose like a small generalissimo addressing her (non-existent) troops. The vultures looked at each other. Then El Condor pointed one feathertip at Jose.

'Wait,' he said. He and Perveen hopped a little away and huddled, conferring with each other behind closed wings.

Jose and Mishi waited. Finally, the vultures seemed to come to an agreement – not without a lot of wing-waving, ruff-ruffling and beak-clacking from Perveen – and returned to face the children.

'His Excellency has decreed,' announced Perveen, looking distinctly unhappy, 'that we will take you as far as we can. Through the myst to the foothills where the River of Time enters the valley. More than that, we cannot do.'

'Oh! Thankyouthankyouthankyou,' rattled Mishi, rushing over to Perveen and flinging her small arms around the vulture's scraggy neck.

'Okay,' Jose said softly. 'Thank you.'

'And then...you're on your own, understand?' said El Condor.

'Understood,' he replied.

'Into Kozitsthereistan,' said El Condor.

'Yes,' said Jose steadily.

El Condor looked from one to the other.

'Jou a bit crazy, keed,' he said to Jose, a lopsided smile twisting his beak. 'I like you.'

'What about me?' said Mishi.

'Jou? Ha!' El Condor let out a bark of laughter. 'Jou *fully* crazy, Mishi. I love *you.*' Which didn't sound, to Jose, as much of a compliment as Mishi seemed to think.

Squatting down on his great, feathered haunches, the big vulture craned his neck back at Jose and cocked his head. 'Well? What are you waiting for?' he said. 'Hop on.'

'Oh dear,' muttered Perveen, as she also hunkered down. 'Only as far as the foothills,' she warned, angling her head backwards to look at Mishi as she scrambled on.

Jose had never ridden a vulture – not many people have – and he was, frankly, terrified. But he thought of his mother, he thought of his father and his little sister, and held fast to a slender, secret idea: that if they managed to find the seed of hope where the River of Time began, then he might – somehow – find his way through Lake Lachrymosa and back to where he belonged.

He clambered onto El Condor's broad back, wrapped his arms around the bird's scraggy neck and buried his face in the (rather tickly) white feathers of his ruff. He tucked his feet behind El Condor's wing pits and clung on for dear death. Once Mishi was similarly positioned, the two birds ran like ungainly chickens and launched themselves into the gloom.

'Whooohoooo!' cried Mishi, whirling one hand in the air.

'Jou cho...choakin' me, keed,' croaked His Excellency, so Jose loosened his grip by a fraction, but kept his eyes tight shut.

When he opened them again, they were soaring out over Lake Lachrymosa. There was no moon and no stars to light their way, and the landscape below them seemed to be etched in Indian ink like a woodcut. Against the dark grey sky Gravepyres appeared as a jumble of squat black boxes, with square pagoda lids stacked one on top of the other. Below them, the water glinted like gunmetal. From this height, Jose could see that the lake was in a far worse state than he'd realised. All around it, the ground lay cracked into a millions tessellations, like a broken mosaic; the water like a patch of smooth glaze on a fired earthen pot.

They flew on over the valley where the river had gouged a course through the hills, and then higher, skimming the bottom of the low, dark clouds. Tendrils of cold air swirled around them, and the ground far below disappeared from view. Enveloped in a gauzy haze, Jose could see nothing beyond the great sweep of El Condor's outstretched wings. He wondered how he knew where they were going, but the great vulture soared steadily on, with occasional beats of his wings, angling the upturned tips to catch invisible currents in the wind and riding them like a surfer might ride the swell of a wave. Perveen and Mishi followed close behind.

With nothing to see but myst, and the steady rush of cool air on his face, Jose slipped into a sort of hypnotic doze. He felt the vulture tilting to the left, soaring in a series of wide circles, drawing a long, lazy spiral in the sky with one elegant fingertip as the ground rose up to meet them.

They landed awkwardly by a dry, stone-strewn gulch. Jose slid over El Condor's head and ended up hanging upside-down from his neck. He let go and flopped down in an ungainly heap. Perveen swooped down in a perfect glide and Mishi slid neatly off her back and landed on her feet.

Dawn was breaking, and the air felt fresh and cold. On the far horizon, impossibly huge, jagged mountain peaks bit into the sky like sharp white teeth.

'Can't you take us any further?' Jose asked, for although he was glad to be back on solid ground, the mountains still looked awfully far away.

'Keed,' said El Condor, stretching his wings and

easing the kinks out of his neck, 'jou need to lose some weight.' He blew out his cheeks.

Perveen was slightly more tactful. 'This is the edge of the no-fly zone: we cannot take you any further.' Then she looked up at the lightening sky. 'We must get back to the Eerie, Your Excellency. Jose, Mishi dear, you're on your own now. All you need to do is follow the riverbed. Remember: stick to the river and you won't get lost. Oh, but do take care,' she said worriedly, looking towards the mountains.

'We will,' Jose reassured her.

The vultures turned, ran, and launched themselves back into the sky.

'Good luck!' cried Perveen over her shoulder.

'*Hasta luego*, keed,' called His Excellency.

'Wait! What...' Jose suddenly shouted. But his words were lost in the wind and the vultures were already out of earshot and soaring away.

Jose looked around. Mishi was standing on a large boulder in the middle of the dry riverbed, looking upstream.

'Right then,' she said.

'Let's go,' said Jose.

And they began to walk.

As they clambered from rock to rock along the riverbed, the sky above them paled and the clouds thinned until they tore in places, like gossamer, and the blue shone through. Colour seemed to leach back into the world. The low, scrubby thorn bushes on either side were covered in tiny, pale green leaflets, dotted here and there with bright yellow blossoms. The pebbles on the riverbed shone smooth – ochre, beige and pale yellow, seal-grey, black or streaked with lines of soft orange – as they trudged along. Larger boulders stood proud, like the humps of great sea creatures cresting above the ground and then plunging back into their own shadows.

At first, Jose kept looking back, half-expecting to see Professor Yama swooping down on them, scythe aloft, or Madam Morte with her hair flying behind her in full Scare mode. Who knew how far Dr Chiplunker could see, scanning the horizon with his telescopic spectacles? Jose and Mishi hurried along, determined to put as much distance between them and Gravepyres as possible. But after a few hours, having seen nothing more dramatic than a butterfly or two, Jose stopped worrying and started to feel a curious sense of elation.

They had done it. They had escaped! They were on their way into Kozitsthereistan. No lessons, no homework, they didn't even have to worry about food – or sleep – or anything at all. All they had to do – as Perveen had said – was follow the river.

He bounded to the top of a large boulder, surveying the land around him like a king. Mishi had stopped to examine a particularly pretty pebble – blueish grey and mottled with white. 'Last one to the top's a pig!' he shouted. She flung the pebble down and scrambled after him, and the two children raced up the slope.

She caught up with him, and they stood together, eyes shining.

'We did it!' said Jose.

'YES!' cried Mishi, punching the air with her fist. Then, hesitantly, 'What did we do?'

Jose rolled his eyes.

'Come on,' he said. And so they did.

By the time the light began to fade from the sky, the excitement had worn off. Jose had twisted his ankle twice on the rocks, and Mishi's tunic was covered in dust. The terrain was growing wilder and more hilly the further they went, and darkness was beginning to fall.

The children decided that there was no point trying to carry on in the dark, and Jose looked around for a place to horizontal. At a bend in the riverbed, a small crescent of sandy shale looked like the perfect place, so Mishi and Jose spread their shawls on the ground and lay down to rest.

The stars came out, one by one at first, and then a multitude, as though someone had flung sequins up into the velvety blackness. It was a little spooky, lying outside in the dark, under the great sweep of starry sky, with not a sound to be heard, but Jose's spirit soared. They were actually on their way. All they had to do was keep following the riverbed and then... well, they'd find the source and get the seed and unblock whatever it was that was stopping the water from flowing (he was a little hazy on this point) and then... the vultures could get through to the Other Side and everything would be... His thoughts faltered at this point, sputtering and dying like an aircraft with engine failure.

All night his mind circled round and round, lifted by thermals of hope, dipping with sudden gusts of doubt.

The next morning dawned clear and pastel blue. Jose stood up and stretched. He looked over to where

Mishi lay, ramrod straight, her arms by her sides as though to attention. She looked so peaceful, and so small. He prodded her shoulder experimentally.

Her eyes flew open and she sat bolt upright.

'Oh, hello,' she said, looking around. 'What are we doing here?'

'Mishi,' said Jose slowly. 'We're on a quest, remember?'

'A quest!' she said, her eyes shining. 'Oooh, that sounds exciting! Come on then.'

She jumped up and started walking down the way they'd come.

'Er, this way...' he said, pointing with his thumb.

'I knew that,' she said, and they carried on upstream.

They walked, and walked, and walked some more.

Jose and Mishi horizontalled when it got dark and got up when it was light. And although the mountains of Kozitsthereistan looked as far away as ever, the terrain grew steadily steeper and wilder, the trees scraggier and more twisted, and the air at night was crisp and cool.

Each day started with Jose reminding Mishi where they were, what they were doing and where they were going, and each time he thought it had finally sunk in, but every morning her face was as blank as ever, as though the night had wiped her mind clean as a blackboard ready for the day's first touch of chalk.

By the fourth or maybe fifth day (it's difficult to keep track of time in the Land of the Dead), Jose's legs were beginning to ache. The wide riverbed of the lower slopes had dwindled to little more than a rock-strewn gully, overarched by dense thickets of bamboo. Willow trees reached down with slender green fingers as if to feel their way to any water that had previously trickled along the bottom. Mishi and Jose battled their way along, jumping from rock to rock, and occasionally scrambling on all fours. It was slow going.

By the sixth (or was it seventh?) day, Jose's feet felt like they'd been pounded to a pulp; he was unable to go any further. He sat down heavily on a rock and eased off his sandals.

'Mishi,' he called. '*Stop!*'

She turned around, surprised. 'Why?'

'I just need to,' he panted, 'I just have to catch my... argh! Mishi! I'm breathing!'

Mishi ran back to him and put her hand on his chest. They watched in awe as it rose and fell.

'Gosh,' she said, her eyes big and round. 'So you are.'

'Are you?' he said.

She put one hand on her tummy and the other on her chest and opened her mouth like a trout. 'Nope,' she said finally. 'I'm fine.'

'That's weird,' said Jose. 'What's happening to me? Am I coming alive, d'you think?'

'I don't think so,' said Mishi, her eyebrows in a straight line. 'That doesn't happen.'

But Jose wasn't so sure. The further they climbed, the less dead he felt. Now, you or I – and even Jose – might suppose that was a good thing, but as they carried on deeper and deeper into the mysterious land of Kozitsthereistan, Jose began to realise there were more disadvantages than you might think. He ran out of breath frequently and, much to Mishi's irritation, they kept having to stop for him to rest. The thorny twigs left painful red welts on his skin – whereas Mishi seemed to brush through them entirely unharmed. And his feet really ached.

But on the plus side, he found his sense of smell coming back: the sharp resinous odour of the pine trees, the delicious scent of wet earth where the river trickled along. As they brushed past lantana bushes, their leaves released into the air that special scent – a heady mix of lemon rind and cut grass. Jose sniffed deeply, welcoming each new smell like a long-lost friend.

Whatever water there had once been had become lost in a mass of reeds and sedge, and the surrounding undergrowth was so tangled and wild there was little to distinguish between the course of the river and the surrounding vegetation. But despite all the greenery it was strangely quiet: not a sound fell on their ears, no twitter of birdsong, no rustle of leaf, no call of a barking deer. Just the sound of four scrambling feet and the steady *huff huff* of Jose's breath.

They were still heading uphill, along a very rocky kind of path, but Jose had the nagging feeling that...

'Where's the river?' he said.

'What river?'

'We're supposed to be following the river, Mishi. That's what Perveen said.'

'We'd better follow it then. Who's Perveen?'

'You know, Perveen. The vulture? The quest we're on...? Gosh, Mishi, what's the matter with you?'

'Nothing's the matter with *me*,' retorted Mishi, huffily. 'I know exACKly where we're going. What's the matter with *you*?'

'???'

'Why don't *you* follow the river, then, if you're so clever.'

'There IS no river!' shouted Jose. 'There's just these stupid, horrid, idiot, stupid rocks, and rocks, and *gah*, ROCKS!' He kicked one just to prove his point, and ended up hopping up and down clutching his foot.

'I *said* we should've gone the other way back there,' said Mishi with an insufferably smug look on her face.

Jose gritted his teeth. 'Okay, fine,' he said and they retraced their steps back to where the riverbed seemed to split into two. Mishi led the way up the left-hand fork and Jose clambered after her. This way seemed even more overgrown but they struggled on until they found the channel ahead totally blocked by a tangled hedge of brambles and a huge fallen tree trunk.

'Where's the river?' said Jose.

'I... um...' Mishi shrugged. 'I don't know.'

'Brilliant,' said Jose sarcastically. 'Happy now?'

Mishi turned round and charged at him, pushing him to the ground with surprising force.

'Don't tell *me* to be happy,' she yelled. 'I'm not happy. You're happy. YOU be happy if you want to be so happy.'

Jose wrestled her off him and then they sat up and looked at each other. Jose had twigs in his hair and a lump of moss on his shoulder. Mishi's tunic was torn and her face was smeared with mud. She glared at him. And then the corner of her mouth twitched. And his did too. And before they knew it, they were laughing like hyenas.

Finally, when the giggles had subsided and Mishi had hiccupped into silence, they lay side by side, looking up at the branches above them.

'We're lost, aren't we?' she said in a small voice.

'Yes,' said Jose.

And then, for a very long time, they didn't say anything at all.

Jose heaved a great sigh – he could, now that he was breathing. It was such a novelty that he sighed again, revelling in the luxury of a long, slow exhale. Then he got to his feet.

'We can't stay here all day,' he said.

The sky above them held a tangerine tinge, and the shadows lengthened. The day had slipped through their fingers, and already the air had a slight chill to it. He looked at the great tangle of branches and twigs in front of them and his mother's voice came back to him: 'If you can't think through it, think around it.'

Dusting himself down, he said, 'We can't get through, so we'll just have to go around.'

He led the way back down a little and then forged off into the undergrowth. Mishi scrambled along behind him, humming a little song, something about hunting a bear…

But after an hour of hard going, they still hadn't found the riverbed. At least we're headed uphill, thought Jose to himself. That must be right, surely? They carried on until Jose could go no further. The muscles in his thighs burned.

By now the light had faded and the first evening star twinkled above the far horizon like a chip of ice. A fresh wind had picked up, blowing down from the mountains, sharpening its blade on the valley sides as it came. Jose tugged his shawl closer around his shoulders.

'We have to find shelter, Mishi.'

Mishi frowned a bit. Such a wimp, she thought to herself. It's not really that cold. But when she looked at him, his arms wrapped around his body, his legs all scratched beneath his tunic, he looked so forlorn that she took pity on him. 'Okay,' she said. 'What about up there?'

She pointed to an opening in the cliff a little way ahead of them, to the right. There was an overhang of rock that looked like it might give them a bit of protection from the wind. They scrambled up the slope and slumped down in the mouth of a cave.

They had barely sat down when they leapt up again. A twig snapped behind them, and Jose whirled around. Oh god! Mishi's song! Maybe they had been on a bear hunt after all! Or they'd stumbled across a bear on a people hunt! Oh god, oh god!

He stood behind Mishi and peered over her shoulder. She took a hesitant step into the cave.

'Hellooo?' said Mishi into the gloom.

'Hellooo?' came an echo. Only it wasn't an echo.

'Wh... who's there?'

'I am,' said the voice. 'Who's *there*?' And then, 'Come in, come in. Aajao.'

They entered the cave. As their eyes adjusted, Mishi and Jose made out the figure of a little old man, bare-bodied and with a long flowing beard, sitting in a lotus position next to a small fire pit. His hair – a tangled mass of thick, twisted dreadlocks – was piled up on his head like a mini-Kozitsthereistani mountainscape, and cast strange shadows on the cave walls by the light of the dancing flames.

'Namaste,' he said, pressing his hands together. He gestured them to sit. 'Myself, Ranjubaba. And you?'

The children namaste-ed him back and introduced themselves.

'Well, well,' said the old man, rubbing his hands together gleefully. 'It's not often I get visitors these days. Are you in search of a boon?'

'A... what?' said Jose.

'A boon, you know. Or a blessing? Mantra? Sacred amulet? Birthstone? Or you need some healing herbs, perhaps? I know them *all*. I don't cast the evil eye anymore, so if that's what you're looking for, you'd better be on your way. Or you just want to take darshan, is that it, hmmm?'

He closed his eyes and composed himself suitably for them to 'take darshan' of him to their hearts' content.

'Sorry, but not really,' explained Jose. 'We're just lost.'

'We're not *just* lost,' frowned Mishi – she didn't want this strange little man to think they were a pair of complete idiots. 'Ackcherly,' she went on importantly, 'we're on a quest.'

'Aha!' The old man's eyes flew open and sparkled brightly. 'I see! A quest for knowledge! For the fruits of eternal wisdom, isn't it? But in order to taste the fruit of enlightenment, first you must smell the flower of earthly experience. Once, there was a cowherd who loved his cows...'

'Thing is,' interrupted Mishi, 'we're looking for something.'

'We are aaaaalll looking for something,' the little man intoned, with a benign smile. 'So the cowherd went to the Buddha and asked...'

'No – she means we're looking for the river,' said Jose quickly, before Ranjubaba could embark again on his confusing talk of fruits and flowers and dairy farming.

'The river?' said Ranjubaba, his head on one side and his hair looking dangerously close to toppling over. 'It is lost?'

'No – I mean, yes. I mean, no. We are.'

'Hmmm,' said Ranjubaba, steepling his fingers.

'See. The River of Time has dried up and the lake is shrinking, so the vultures can't get through to the Land of the Living, and we need to find the source and unblock the river so that El Condor can fly Jose back to his family and not be dead no more,' said Mishi. Jose looked at her, amazed. That was the most sense she had ever made!

'Ah, family,' Ranjubaba sighed. 'I, too, once had a family. All gone, all gone.' And he looked so sad, Jose instinctively put a hand on the old man's bony knee.

'What happened?' he asked.

'Oh-ho, long story,' said Ranjubaba, patting Jose's hand and immediately brightening up. 'They wanted me to stay in the plains and follow my father's calling. Me! In the import-export garment business, can you imagine? But I knew my destiny lay elsewhere. I was cast out: the black sheep of the family. But, of course, you must be knowing the song?'

The children looked blank.

'Baba? The black sheep?'

'Baa baa, black sheep – that's you?'

The old man nodded modestly. Then waved his hands in the air and grinned. 'But that's all water under the hedge. Since attaining moksha I am no longer troubled by such worldly concerns. I am detached. Supremely and utterly unaffected by good or ill or... *aaaaaaarrrrghgh!*' He suddenly shrieked and leapt up, brushing his hair frantically. 'Spider. Brrrr,' he shivered.

Jose and Mishi looked at each other, nonplussed. It seemed that Ranjubaba was not, perhaps, quite as detached as he would have them believe.

'I have studied the ancient shastras and ayurvedic texts,' he went on, now happily spider-free. 'My Guruji only had to look at my palm once – once! – and he saw my destiny. My thumbs are green.' He waggled them at the children helpfully. (They looked like perfectly ordinary brown thumbs to Mishi and Jose – though he really could do with a nail cut).

Then he dug into a small cloth bag that lay next to him. 'Look,' he said, holding out a fistful of what looked like spices. 'Seeds.' Ranjubaba poked them about with one bony finger. 'Blue poppy. Jeera. Phlox. Forget-me-lots. Each one,' he held one up to the flickering firelight, 'contains a forest. Each lotus,' he held another delicately in his fingers, 'a thousand lotuses...'

'Babaji – er, sir,' Jose leaned forward eagerly, 'it's a wonderful collection, really it is. But do you – would you, by any chance, have a seed of hope?'

Ranjubaba rocked back on his heels and looked puzzled.

'Seed of...?' And then his face cleared. 'Ah, you are talking of the *shraddha beej*, I think. Hope, yes, perhaps – a little loose translation, perhaps "faith" is better. Or "confidence" or...'

'But do you have one?' blurted out Jose.

'That is a rare and precious thing, children. Very rare...'

'So – you *don't* have one?'

'Er... no. Not as such. I have some lovely acorns though.' He held out a handful.

Mishi took one, to be polite.

'According to the *Sushsruta Samita*,' the old man went on, 'the shraddha beej can only be found where the River of Time begins...'

'Yes! That's it!' Jose's face lit up. 'The Eternal Spring! That's where we need to go. Can you help us? Do you know the way?'

'Can I? Do I?' Ranjubaba pressed one side of his nose and snorted deeply. 'As the Great Sage Vyasa said, "Can you step in the same stream twice?" Can you tell where one moment ends and the next begins? What comes up must come down! Does the Pope... Oh, never mind. We must go with the flow! And if you can't go *with* the flow, because there *is* no flow, well then, my friends, we must go against it! Tomorrow, we will start!'

The children really had no idea what the strange little man was going on about, but he himself seemed entirely happy with the explanation, and promptly lay down and started to snore.

Night had fallen by this time, and the mountains lay silent under the sparkling sky. There was nothing more they could do that day, and they were glad of the warmth and the shelter of the cave. The children spread their shawls on the ground, lay down and closed their eyes as the fire dwindled to a pile of glowing embers and outside, the icy stars wheeled slowly above.

'Wake up, Jose.'

His eyes flew open.

It was his mother.

'Come on, beta – you'll be late for school.'

Jose scrambled out of bed. Sunlight was pouring into his bedroom, and his school uniform lay at the foot of the bed. He dressed quickly and went to the dining room. A bowl of Chocos stood ready for him and his father was sitting there with his morning mug of chai. Jose ran his hand over his father's bald head, and his father retaliated by ruffling Jose's mass of curls. Then he caught his son up in a bear hug and Jose laughed and squirmed at the ticklish scratching of his father's beard on his neck.

Jose grabbed his bag from the back of the chair and ran to the veranda. His mother stood in the doorway, with Surya on one hip. 'Water bottle?' she said. He took it from her and slung the strap over his shoulder.

'Tiffin?'

'Got it! Bye!' He waved with one hand as he ran towards the bus stop.

In the lane, Blackie and Raja, the colony dogs, were lying around; the stray cats were nosing around a pile of rubbish near the gate; the crows were going *caw-caw-caw* and underneath everything was the familiar rumble of traffic.

When the school van drew up, Jose was mildly surprised to see that it was not his usual van but a small carriage – like a rollercoaster cart – and there was just room for him and the driver, Ram Narayan, to sit side by side. Ram Narayan pulled the curved safety bar down onto their laps and they set off towards a large, dark archway. The rails they were travelling on led inside and swiftly dropped into a steep spiral. 'Hold tight, beta,' the driver grinned as they shot through the tunnel. They were heading underground, the walls were so close, Jose felt like he couldn't breathe, he was being shaken and rocked from side to side...

'Wake up, wake up!'

His eyes flew open.

It was Mishi.

Jose sat up and looked around, blinking. The dream had been so vivid, he felt sick and giddy.

'I was drea...' he started to say, but Mishi was already at the cave entrance and heading out into the light.

Outside, Ranjubaba was upside-down, balancing on his head, his hair swirled on the ground like a matted tangle of grey rope and his flat feet seeming to hold up the bright blue sky. As Jose emerged from the cave, Ranjubaba jack-knifed slowly down and then kind of unfolded himself backwards until he was standing up straight again. He beamed and spun around, lifting his arms to the sunlit air.

'Chalo! Chalo!' he said. 'Time to go!'

'Go?' said Jose, still a bit dazed.

'The quest!' beamed Ranjubaba. 'You have not forgotten your purpose, I hope?'

'He,' said Mishi pointedly, 'never forgets *anything*. Come on, Joe,'

'– *Jose* –' said Jose, rolling his eyes.

'I mean Jose. We have to find the river, remember?'

Jose looked at her in surprise but said nothing.

'Ranjubaba's going to show us the way,' she said, smiling.

Ranjubaba went back into the cave, sprinkled a handful of dust over the embers of the fire. He put a small tin saucepan, a cracked plate and a small, rather dirty glass into his cloth bag, folded up the shawl on which he'd been sleeping and tucked it on top. Then he slung the bag across his bare body, retied his loincloth firmly, and took Mishi's hand. 'To the river,' he declared, then added in a more serious tone, 'you must see it for yourselves.'

The three companions set off up the mountainside: Ranjubaba leading the way, Mishi next, and Jose bringing up the rear. It was a steep climb. The children's feet kept slipping on the scree, sending flurries of pebbles and sand cascading down the valley, but the old man skipped along as surefooted as a mountain goat. Every now and then he would stop, bend down and pick a few leaves or flowers to stuff into his bag.

The air was as clear as glass and the sky arched over everything, a limpid aquamarine blue, the kind that you only get high up in the mountains. The tracing-paper skies of Gravepyres seemed a lifetime ago and a world away to Jose. The last wisps of his dream had blown away, and he lifted his face to the sky: the sun like a warm hand cupping his cheek. Now they had Ranjubaba to guide them, he felt sure that they'd find the river and carry on up to the source. He wondered what might be blocking the river – and he was reminded of another of his grandfather's favourite sayings: 'We'll cross that bridge when we come to it.' That was it! Maybe it was, in fact, a bridge that had collapsed or something. Whatever it was, he was sure they'd be able to fix it. And with that happy thought he carried on, with a spring in his step.

Mishi had skipped a little way ahead of them, and Ranjubaba had stopped to pick some herbs. Plucking up courage, Jose decided to ask him something. After all, he was a sadhu – a wise man – and had spent so much time in the mountains... maybe he'd know.

'Babaji?'

'My child?'

'I've been wondering. The thing is that... well, I know I'm dead and everything. I mean – I thought I was. I... it's just that now, I'm not so sure.'

'Yes?' said Ranjubaba, straightening up.

'Well, it's just that this morning I had a dream, I think, which means I must have been asleep – like properly asleep, not just horizontalling. And look,' he formed his mouth into a little 'o' and blew on his hand, 'I can breathe a bit too. So... maybe... I was thinking, then maybe I might be alive, and if I am alive – even a little bit – then maybe I would be able to... um... go back home...and...' His voice trailed off.

Ranjubaba looked at the leaf he was holding between his thumb and forefinger, and rubbed it thoughtfully. Then he looked at Jose and said, 'Kozitsthereistan is a strange land, Jose. It affects people differently. Some love it here. Others go quite maaaad.' He waved his hands around and rolled his eyes. Then he gathered himself together and gave a little cough. 'Personally, I love it,' he said, just to be clear. 'Yet, who can understand its mysteries? I cannot say. I have lived here many a year, and my

Guruji before me and his before him, and yet the sum total of aaaall our wisdom would not fill this single little leaf. What we think we know is soooo little. But what we *know* we don't is,' and here he pirouetted around, arms outstretched, taking in the whole landscape, his eyes alight, 'soooo vast.'

'Are *you* dead?' Jose said, thinking that in any other circumstances this would have been a very odd thing to ask.

'Me, child? No, no, no...' said Ranjubaba, shaking his head.

'But...' Jose began again, but the old man silenced him with a hand.

'Jose, still your mind. Think. The first part of "question" is...?'

'Erm... quest?'

'YES!' the old man cried. 'It begins with a *quest* – remember? It ends with "eon".' He carried on with a small frown, 'But never mind about that. The point is, you cannot go back – only forwards. Onwards and upwards. Chalo,' he concluded with a clap of his hands, 'Mishi is waiting.'

It was late afternoon as they scrambled up to the summit of a large hill and finally hauled themselves over the peak. The children gasped, awestruck, at the vista beyond. The hills rose up on either side of a deep valley, lushly wooded on both sides in stark contrast to the rocky, dusty terrain they had left behind. The treetops on the far side were gilded by the low rays of the setting sun, but their side was already in deep shade.

Ranjubaba pointed down at a thin ribbon of silver snaking its way through the gorge. 'There is the river.' And then added, almost to himself, 'At least, what's left of it.'

They set off down the slope through the darkening wood.

Night had almost fallen when they finally reached the bottom. The trees stopped abruptly and they emerged onto the wide valley floor. They hopped from rock to rock until they reached the river, if you could call it that. A thin trickle of water gurgled gently over the pebbles and gathered in small, still pools behind larger rocks, glinting silver in the fading light. Mishi, the smallest among them, could easily hop across it without even getting her toes wet.

Ranjubaba squatted down and dipped his fingers in the icy water. 'All that is left of the River of Time,' he sighed, and dabbed a droplet on each child's forehead in a sort of wistful blessing.

'But what's stopping it?' said Jose. 'Do you think it might be a bridge that's fallen down? Or is it...' He suddenly remembered something from his Social Studies textbook at school. '...is it something to do with climate change?'

Ranjubaba's eyes were sad and dark. 'Oh, Jose,'

he sighed, 'if only it were that simple.' He reached out a hand to help him across.

Puzzled, the children followed as Ranjubaba led them along the far side of the river. After some time they heard noises – creaking, clanging, chugging noises – that seemed to be coming from somewhere upstream. Then Jose smelt something, a sour harsh note that cut through the sweet scent of pine.

'What...?'

Ranjubaba looked back and put a bony finger to his lips. They crept onwards, trying not to make a sound, until they rounded a bend – and Jose almost cried out in shock.

A massive wall towered over them, stretching from high up on one side of the valley across to the other. It was absolutely gigantic, cutting the sky in half, looming over them as though it were about to topple over and swallow them up. They could make out the bustle of activity, and heard the low hum of machinery and the juddering cough of a generator. High up, cranes and diggers were silhouetted against the twilit sky, like alien insects waving their claws, and the children heard the vicious whine of a chainsaw and the sickening crash of a tree as it splintered and fell to the forest floor.

'What is it?' whispered Mishi, eyes round as saucers.

'That, my child, is the Dam,' said Ranjubaba softly, and beckoned them into the forest.

The children followed Ranjubaba up the slope and through the woods. They emerged near the top where a chain-link fence ran around the construction site. Arc lights bathed the area in a sickly helium glow. Men in orange jackets and heavy black boots were signalling up to the crane operator, and as the children watched, the crane arm swung a menacing hook high over their heads like a massive inverted question mark.

They instinctively ducked down and froze. It was just as well they did, as the trees, just where their heads would have been, were raked with a searchlight. They stayed crouched as the crunch of boots came closer and then stopped. A man dropped a heavy toolbox on the ground and rummaged around inside it. He straightened up and began to unscrew something in a switchbox halfway up one of the perimeter posts.

Then another man – similarly dressed in dark blue overalls and wearing a yellow hardhat – came clumping over. The men stood not six feet from where the children and Ranjubaba were, and their words could be heard clearly.

'Are you done yet?' said the second man.

'Yah, just about. Gimme a minute.'

A cigarette flared in the darkness.

'Ah, get on with it, can't ya? I'm starving.'

'Oy, the fuse's blown on the generator – again. No rest for us tonight: boss's orders. We're already be'ind schedule.'

'Huh, no overtime, you can bet on that. 'Snot our fault the bloomin' generator's bust. But it's our pay that gets cut, innit?'

'That should hold it,' said the first man, gruffly. He gave a final twist of the screwdriver, closed the door of the switchbox and bent down to pack up his tools. 'Try it now.'

The other man said something into his walkie-talkie. And with a great creaking roar, like some dragon waking up, a generator burst into life. A huge neon sign flickered on over the main building:

PLASTICORP

WITH YOU. FOR YOU. ALWAYS.

'Righto,' said the second man. 'Let's call it a day.'

As the scrunch of boots faded away, the children

and Ranjubaba stood slowly and crept along the side of the fence, keeping to the darkness of the trees.

On the far side of the Dam, a great black lake lay across the valley. It stretched away in a vast, elongated triangle, pierced here and there by dead trees, their branches raised to the sky like white skeletal arms. Unlike Lake Lachrymosa, which shone like a bright mirror, the reservoir reflected nothing. It was as dense and opaque as a lid.

They tramped along in silence, each caught up in his or her own thoughts. The roar of the generator gradually faded to a distant rumble and the still, silent night took over once more. Finally, they came to a halt. Ranjubaba took a large shawl out of his bag and unrolled it on the ground. He sat down next to Mishi. Jose went down to the edge of the reservoir and looked out across the dark water. In the distance, the lights of the construction site glowed eerily, like a yellow stain at the edge of the sky. Well, he thought bleakly, at least they now knew what was stopping the river from flowing. He could almost hear El Condor's scornful voice: 'No-brain, meat-poisoning, concrete-loving uglifiers.' Jose had never felt particularly proud of belonging to the human race – he'd never, honestly, given it much thought. But just now he felt downright ashamed of his own species.

He went and sat down with the others.

'Babaji,' said Mishi in a small voice. 'What's Plasticorp? What do they do? What's the Dam for?'

Ranjubaba placed a hand on her head and sighed a long, bitter sigh. Then he started to speak. At first haltingly, and then with more and more fluidity, he told them how one day, when he was out gathering herbs in the forest, he had heard a great rending and screeching sound as a huge drill burst through the side of the mountain. All the birds flew up in a great cloud, and the forest was filled with their terrified alarm calls. He climbed a tree and watched from the branches as, out through the gash in the mountain came men and machines – diggers and earthmovers, steel rods and concrete mixers. 'They poured through like ants from a hole,' he said. Each day, he would come and watch until... 'I couldn't watch it anymore.' A tear leaked from one eye and made its way down his cheek and into his beard. 'The birds started to disappear, the animals too – I was afraid. And then they started to build the Dam and the river became small, so small. I thought the world would end. I tried meditating. I blessed them! Blessed them – as only that can truly heal...'

'But Babaji, who are they?' said Mishi.

The old man seemed to struggle to answer.

'Plasticorp,' he spat as though the very word tasted foul in his mouth. 'Pah! They want to stop the flow, and package it up, and sell it on. Make pots of money, no matter what the cost. They are eating up everything in the forest to build that Dam, and they won't stop until they've killed us all. Blast them! I mean bless them, the nasty little rakshas, may they be safe and warm and loved and respected.' And muttering to himself, he turned away.

Jose and Mishi sat side by side, looking out across the dark, dead water.

'Now what do we do?' said Mishi.

'We carry on,' he said. 'Look, all this water has to come from somewhere, right? So we just need to find where it enters the reservoir, and follow it upstream. We have to find the source.'

'But what for?' insisted Mishi. 'Why do we have to go to the source? The river can't flow because of that horrid thing.' She gestured back at the Dam. '*That's* the problem. We have to go back and *tell* someone. Professor Yama will know what to do. We've got to do *something*!'

'What can we do?' said Jose, his voice hard. He didn't have laser-beam eyes that could burn through concrete, or a Spiderman suit that would give him stupendous strength or even a couple of sticks of dynamite he could hurl... He had one little girl, and a mad old hermit.

'Look,' he carried on in a more conciliatory tone, 'we will go back and tell them, I promise, but first we have to find the source – the Eternal Spring. Houri McClury told me about it. I need to get a seed of hope or shraddha beej or whatever it was that Ranjubaba called it, and that's at the Eternal Spring.' He neglected to mention that Houri had said that the seed wasn't actually real. 'Because once we've got that...'

Jose's voice faltered. Because then, he wanted to say, he could go back home. He could undo what had been done, catch the wail of horror that had issued from his mother's mouth, stuff it back, rewind Time itself, undo a dreadful wrong, make things right again. Somehow, in his mind, the black bats of despair that fled from her open mouth could be vanquished by the shining rays of light that radiated from the seed that he'd seen in the illustrated Herbarium. That was the straw he held on to so tightly, drowning as he was: that the seed's light was the equal and opposite of the sound of black despair.

'I... I know it's not much to go on,' he concluded sadly, 'but it's all that we have.'

Now he had shown them the Dam and refound the 'lost' river, Ranjubaba was all ready to go back, but it was Mishi – surprisingly – who explained, really quite coherently, the reasons for going on. At the thought of finding a new seed, and particularly one as rare and coveted as this, Ranjubaba's eyes positively sparkled. He insisted, even though neither of them actually objected, that he carry on with them, and the children were delighted.

'The Eternal Spring,' he said, a note of wonder in his voice. 'My Guruji's guruji would speak of it. I have never been that far. Oh, surely this will be a grand quest, my children.'

They rested for a few hours and started off before dawn, anxious to put as much distance as possible between themselves and the Plasticorp Dam. As the sky lightened, minute by minute, they trudged silently along the side of the still, dark waters of the reservoir, leaving a trail of dark footprints in the dewy grass.

No more was said about Plasticorp's work. But the Dam cast a long shadow over the three companions and try as he might to dismiss it from his thoughts, Jose couldn't. Why was the Dam there anyway? It was just so *wrong*. It didn't belong here, that great ugly thing. But what could they do? If Professor Yama and all the teachers at Gravepyres hadn't been able to do anything, there was clearly nothing that *could* be done. The Dam stood in his mind like a great blank barrier, drying up the words in his throat, stopping his thoughts in their tracks. He resolutely put one foot in front of the other, head down.

The sun was past its zenith as they finally approached the end of the reservoir, when Mishi suddenly stopped and held up her hand.

'What's that?' she said.

And then they heard it: the tinkling, gurgling murmur of running water.

'The river!' announced Ranjubaba.

'The river!' breathed Jose.

'It sounds like a river,' said Mishi, and she ran towards the sound.

In fact, it wasn't much more than a stream: a thin ribbon of crystal clear water that came tripping and sparkling down the mountainside and was swallowed with barely a ripple by the reservoir's dark water. Mishi knelt down and cupped her hands in the water. It was icy cold, fresh and clear. She splashed some on her face and laughed. The heaviness that Jose had felt near the Dam seemed to lift from his shoulders. He slipped off his shoes and stood ankle-deep on the pebbles and sand at the bottom, feeling the water caress his toes. He kicked a spray of water at Mishi and she splashed him back. Ranjubaba settled down on the grassy bank in full lotus position, an expression of Deep Peace on his face, as the children laughed and splashed each other until they both fell down, exhausted and exhilarated, on the carpet of fresh grass.

Just being near the river seemed as good as a full night's sleep. Refreshed, the three travellers got to their feet and started off again.

'Onwards and upwards, my friends,' said Ranjubaba gaily, 'onwards and upwards!'

XV

With the Dam far behind them and the river at their feet, Jose felt much happier. Now they were truly in the mountains. The sunlight slanted down, sparkling on spiders' webs that hung beneath the trees like diamond necklaces. The air was fresh and cool, scented with deodar and cedar, and the ground beneath their feet was a thick carpet of fragrant pine needles, dotted here and there in the shadows mushrooms that glowed like moonstones.

The riversides were bursting with fiddle fern and blue poppies, purple anemones and buttercups. They walked beneath grand cathedral arches of bamboo, each leaf like a single brushstroke of lime-green paint. Down by the edges of the stream, the grass was short and tender, strewn with clover and plump cushions of star-moss. For the first time, Jose and Mishi heard the twitter of birdsong – the low cooing of a pigeon, the knocking of a woodpecker – and the *chip-chip-chip* of squirrels up in the branches. At one point, Ranjubaba stopped to point out the tracks in the mud left by tragopan and ptarmigan. At another, the deep scrapings of wild boar, the broken branches of a bush where a bear had been foraging for berries. They glimpsed a red fox in a tree, its black eyes rimed with white fur as though it was wearing spectacles.

The trees here were unlike any others that Jose had seen. Shaggy with trailing moss and lichen, their trunks were white and hollow, made of delicate capillaries like crocheted lace, knot-holes like the eye sockets of birds' skulls. 'Ossiferous pine,' said Ranjubaba. 'Very ancient.'

'How much further?' Jose groaned. His feet were killing him – or would have if he weren't already dead.

Ranjubaba was bending down to pick some strange coral-like fungi that poked like tiny orange fingers from the base of a fallen tree trunk. He stuffed them in his bag, which was by now bulging with all the plants and leaves he'd been collecting along the way. He looked even odder than he normally did, as he had decorated his long, tangled beard with small white flowers.

'Oh ho!' laughed the old man, looking up at him. 'Far, far and away, little one. Lots more to go, don't you worry!'

'Can we rest for a while?' pleaded Jose. 'My feet!'

'Look,' said Mishi, 'there's a clearing up ahead. We can stay there for the night.'

So they did.

The next day was the same – except steeper and colder. By nightfall they had climbed hundreds of feet up from the valley, and the wind cut like a knife. It moaned through the hollow pines, playing them like bone-flutes. They took shelter in a cave next to a small stream, and the children foraged for twigs and leaves for Ranjubaba to make a fire with. He rubbed a twig between his palms on a small knot-hole in a broken branch and blew on the sparks. Soon they had a delicious fire going, and only a little bit of Ranjbaba's beard got singed – not that you could tell, actually, because the whole thing was so salt-and-peppery and frizzy. Mishi didn't seem to feel the cold, but Jose stretched his hands towards the dancing flames, grateful for the warmth.

From his bag Ranjubaba took out a little pan and set it on the flames. He tossed in a few seeds and a handful of grains from a pouch, and while they were roasting and popping, he took the small glass tumbler down to the stream to fill it with water. This he added to the pan.

'Ah,' said Ranjubaba contentedly, stirring the contents with a stick. 'Life is good.'

Perhaps, thought Jose, I would feel the same, if only I could eat. But he felt nothing in his belly:

he could barely remember what 'hunger' felt like. He just ached in every muscle from his ears to his toenails.

Having licked his fingers clean, Ranjubaba wrapped his shawl around his skinny body and positioned himself at the mouth of the cave. 'I'll sit on watch,' he said. 'You never know...'

'Never know? Never know what?' said Jose nervously.

'Oh well,' Ranjubaba replied airily, 'snow leopards... bears... mountain lions...'

'Lions?! You mean we might get... *eaten*?'

'No, no, no,' smiled Babaji. 'No, no... well, yes, I suppose, maybe. But that's why I'm on watch, na? You know, Jose, sometimes I think you are bit glass-half-empty.'

Jose frowned. 'What do you mean?'

Ranjubaba uncrossed his legs and went quickly down to the stream again with the glass tumbler. He came back and put it on the ground in front of Jose. 'Full?' he asked.

Jose nodded.

Ranjubaba drank some of the water. 'And now?' he said, putting the glass down again.

'Well, that's obvious,' said Jose. 'It's half empty.'

The old man's face split into a wide smile, like he'd just proved his point.

'Ah,' he said, 'but maybe it is not. To an optimist, it is still half full!' He threw the rest of the water out into the darkness and tapped the glass on the ground. '*Now* it is fully empty,' he cackled.

'No it's not,' said Mishi.

'It is,' said Jose, crossly. This was a stupid conversation.

'It's *not*,' insisted Mishi.

'Yes it *is*,' said Jose, and just to be sure, he took the glass from Ranjubaba, shook it upside down and thrust it at her.

Mishi held it carefully in both hands. 'It's completely full,' she said, 'it's just full of air.'

At this, Ranjubaba clapped his hands together and whooped. He scooped up the glass and held it high over his head. 'And look – now the empty glass is full of night!'

'Now you're just being ridiculous,' said Jose as his companions tossed the glass back and forth. 'Mind you don't spill any,' laughed Mishi. 'Catch!' 'Whoops!'

When they had finally giggled themselves out, Ranjubaba set some more water to boil and rummaged in his bag for peppermint leaves to make tea. Mishi lay down on her shawl, little eruptions of laughter shaking her body from time to time. And Jose, half-hoping a mountain lion *would* come along in the night and carry them both off, curled up, back to the fire, and fell into an uneasy sleep, dreaming of claws and teeth.

The following morning dawned bright and crisp. Jose looked about the cave – he was alone. Fearing that his ill-humour had, in fact, summoned a hungry lion while he slept, he hurried to the mouth of the cave and looked out. Babaji was standing with one leg bent, the other stretched out behind, his back arched. One arm curved up in front of him, the other stretched behind. Mishi was standing next to him, hands on hips.

'What's that one then?' she said.

He looked down at her, his face crinkling with a smile. 'Gentle warrior,' he said.

Mishi tried copying him, her knees bent and her arms waving about in the air. She looked highly unstable.

'Oopsie,' said Ranjubaba, catching her as she toppled sideways.

They looked up and saw Jose. 'Oh, it's you,' said Mishi.

Well – duh, thought Jose, who did she *think* it was? But he just answered, 'Yes, everything alright?'

'We're doing jo-ga,' said Mishi, unnecessarily.

'O-kay,' said Jose. 'Oooh, it's c-cold.'

Mishi pointed at him. 'Ranjubaba, look, look!' she said. 'He looks like a steam train!'

She was right. It was cold enough to see his breath.

'Haaaaaah,' he went, 'haa haa haaaaah. Hey

Mishi, I'm Cloudforming! I wish Madame Cecelia could see this!'

Mishi danced around him. Then she stopped in front of Ranjubaba and frowned. 'Why can't I do that?' she asked him.

Ranjubaba smiled. 'You can – can't you? Jose here tells me you're the best cloudformer in the whole school.'

'That's not what I mean.'

Ranjubaba tugged his beard a little, sending a few petals from the small white flowers drifting down. 'Mishi – you are, well, you are a very, very special girl,' he said. 'In fact,' he went on, 'I'm not sure I've ever met anyone quite like you.'

'Because I can't breathe?' she said.

'No.'

'Cos... I know so much stuff?'

'No.'

'Cos... I'm so pretty?'

Jose snorted.

'No – although you very are,' Ranjubaba added hastily. Then he cupped her face in his hands, and tilted her head up. He scanned her face like he was searching for something – something hidden, something very precious. 'You remind me so much of my Guruji,' he said, almost to himself. 'So much in the here, so much of the now. So very *present*.'

Shaking his head with a mix of what seemed

132

like bewilderment and wonder, he released her, shouldered his bag, and straightened up. He scanned the far horizon where a mass of steely grey cloud was gathering.

'We'd better be going. Looks like snow.'

By the time they reached a high pass, a few flakes had begun to drift down. It was bitterly cold and Jose wrapped his arms around himself as they walked along, wondering just how much further they had to go. Far below, carving its way through a deep gorge, the river wound its way along, its waters here a pale jade-green, foaming white as it crashed past boulders.

'Aren't you cold?' Mishi asked Ranjubaba.

'Me?' he cried, 'not at all! I dry wet sheets on my bare body with the inner fire of *prana*.'

'Oh,' said Mishi, although she secretly wondered why, if his prana – or whatever – was so toasty, his teeth were chattering so much.

They were making their way through a forest of ossiferous pine when Ranjubaba signalled them to stop. There was something in the trees up ahead. Something making muffled, struggly animal noises.

The children followed Ranjubaba nervously, Jose's head full of bears, mountain lions and snow leopards. He felt Mishi slip her small cold hand into his. They crept to the edge of a clearing. And then they stopped, dead.

Jose clapped a hand to his mouth.

Dangling from the treetops above the clearing was a strange contraption: a triangular steel frame suspended from the branches by a pulley, with a tangle of netting hanging down, and in the midst of the netting something small and orange and furry was hooting and grunting.

'What is it?' whispered Mishi.

'It's trapped, whatever it is,' replied Jose.

'Poor thing,' said Ranjubaba.

'Well – don't just stand there. We have to get it down,' cried Mishi, springing into action. Ranjubaba stood beneath the net, Jose scrambled on to his shoulders and stood as high as he could reach – still not quite high enough. So then Mishi climbed on top – with a lot of 'ow's and 'mind my hair's from Ranjubaba – and sat on Jose's shoulders. With difficulty, she managed to untangle the animal from the netting and haul it out. The little creature clung on to Mishi for dear life as she descended, rather ungracefully, just as Ranjubaba's shaking knees gave out.

Three humans and one small creature fell to the forest floor in a huge flump and sat looking at each other. The creature looked rather like a baby orangutan. It had long arms and thick orangey-red fur. Its button-bright eyes peered at them curiously from its black face, and its leathery fingers explored their clothes and hair with surprising gentleness. It made little clicking noises with its tongue, blinked its big round eyes and hooted at them quizzically.

'Hello, little monkey,' said Jose. 'Awww, it's so *cute*.'

The creature clambered up onto Ranjubaba's shoulders and rummaged through his dreadlocks in search of tasty titbits.

'Eeeee, that tickles!' Ranjubaba laughed, squirming.

Then Jose noticed a strange smell wafting over the clearing. It smelt of wild garlic… and rotten egg with a hint of wet dog, and something a bit… erm…

'Peee-ew! Mishi, did you…?'

Mishi shook her head vigorously, looking highly offended.

Jose sniffed the air again. Actually, now that he came to think of it, it wasn't so bad after all. In fact, it smelled a bit like his mother's talcum powder, or… or cut grass and long summer afternoons… with a hint of something citrusy and fresh… In fact, it was the most wonderful smell he'd ever smelled in his whole life. A dreamy look came over his face.

The little creature's nose twitched and its ears flapped. It hooted gleefully and took off at a mad lolloping run into the trees.

'Wait! Come back h…' Mishi started. And then stopped. And stared. 'Uh-oh,' she said.

Out of the forest, lumbering towards them, came a huge, hairy *thing*. It seemed to push the trees aside, like a man walking through elephant grass. It was covered in shaggy brown fur, with enormous arms hanging down almost as long as its body.

Mishi scrambled to her feet and backed away very slowly.

Jose, on the other hand, didn't seem the least bothered. 'Oh, this is a nice place for a picnic,' he said happily, looking round the clearing. He sat down on a tussock and began to pick some of the tiny star-like alpine flowers that dotted the ground. Ranjubaba strolled over to where Jose was sitting. 'Yes, yes,' he said, settling down next to him. 'Flowers are so lovely, na?'

'Ranjubaba!!! What are you doing??' squeaked Mishi. This was really no time to be messing around with flowers! They were in imminent danger of being crushed to a pulp or eaten by an enormous hairy monster and there they were making daisy chains!

The creature took a step into the clearing, crushing a huge patch of grass, its footprint the size of a sofa. Mishi screamed. The ground shook as the creature dropped down on all fours. Then it opened its huge mouth and let out a deafening roar that echoed across the valley, sending a small avalanche of scree skittering down into the gorge. The baby had clambered up onto its mother's back and was hooting like this was all a great game.

'Thunder,' said Jose, jumping up. 'I love storms.' He picked up a pinecone and waved it at Mishi. 'Want to play catch?'

'Ooh, here! Here!' Ranjubaba gestured to Jose to toss the pinecone across.

Mishi was ready to scream again – partly out of sheer terror, but mostly out of utter frustration with her useless companions. Luckily, the monster, perhaps deciding that there were tastier options in the forest that these three little mouthfuls (at least one of which looked like it might be rather tough and stringy under all that hair), turned and lumbered away, disappearing into the trees with the baby clinging to its back.

As the strange smell cleared, so did her friends' faces. Jose fumbled a catch, and then picked up the pinecone from the ground and looked at it, puzzled. Then he noticed Mishi standing frozen beneath the tree. 'What are you...' He looked around. 'Where's the...' Then he stopped again. 'Erm. What just happened?'

'You!' yelled Mishi. 'You went all pickewlier!'

'Me? Did not!' he retorted.

'Yes, you did! You wanted to have a *picnic!* With a great big YETI breathing down our necks!'

'Picnic? Are you crazy? Did you say *yeti*?' Jose looked around, alarmed.

Then Mishi turned on Ranjubaba, who had a daisy chain on his head and was looking slightly dazed.

'And as for YOU,' she cried, her eyes sparking fire. 'YOU and your f... flippin' f... flowers!'

She launched herself at his middle and started hitting him – not very hard, mind you. Ranjubaba fended off her little fists, and then enveloped her in a hug as she buried her head in his beard and sobbed uncontrollably. When she had finally calmed down, Ranjubaba fished a piece of cloth from his bag for her to blow her nose on.

'A yeti?' said Jose. 'Are you sure?'

'Of course I'm sure. Didn't you see? It was absolutely ENORMOUS.'

Jose frowned. Now he thought about it, he had vaguely noticed a big creature arriving in the glade: it just hadn't seemed particularly worth bothering about just then. What had been very clear and very important was just how very nice it would be to have a game of pinecone-catch at exactly at that moment.

Ranjubaba had gone over to where the monster had entered the clearing and was kneeling down where its huge foot had crushed the grass. Then he sprang over to a tree nearby and examined the trunk. A tuft of russet fur had caught in the bark. He picked it out carefully with his fingers and thumb, and then lifted it to his nose and sniffed.

'Notyeti,' he said, his eyes slightly unfocussed.

'What do you mean?' cried Mishi. 'It was too a yeti – I saw it!'

'Notyeti,' repeated Ranjubaba with awe in his voice. 'It was a notyeti.' He whirled around suddenly, his face shining. 'I knew it!' he cried. 'I knew it! My Guruji is the only person to have ever encountered one: but when he came down from the mountains, no one believed him. A hoaxer, they called him – faker! Fabulist! Madman! Teller of tall tales and soggy bog stories. Ha! But I believed him. I always knew!'

'But why couldn't you see it, Babaji?' said Mishi, her eyebrows knitted together. 'Why did you both go all pickewlier?'

'Ah, the scent of the notyeti – so Guruji told – it *does* things to a person.'

'But... but then... why didn't I...?

Ranjubaba looked at her, an unreadable look in his kind, brown eyes. 'You, Mishi,' he said, 'you are a little bit different, perhaps. You are... a rather special case, I think.' He put his hand on her head briefly. And then he looked up at the sky. 'Come,' he said, slinging his bag over his shoulder, 'looks like there's a storm coming.'

Ranjubaba was not wrong. The peaks above them were already shrouded in clouds and the snow began to come down thick and fast, swirling in front of their eyes and dusting the tops of the ossiferous pine as white as their trunks. Fat flakes danced before their eyes, settling on Ranjubaba's beard and eyelashes. Soon, the only colour in this wide, white landscape were two dots of ochre-orange: Mishi and Jose, clutching their tunics about them, heads bent against the bitter wind. Slipping and stumbling on icy rocks, they clambered over a ridge, and came face to face with a huge bank of frozen ice that stretched across the valley below. Ranjubaba pointed wordlessly to a rocky overhang on the side of the cliff, his grey-white flag of beard streaming out behind him. They trudged on, following in his deepening footsteps, leaning into the wind like three tiny italics on a vast white page.

Ranjubaba held out his hand for Jose and hauled him into the lee of the rocks. He did the same for Mishi, and the three of them huddled together out of the wind that moaned and keened past them like a soul in torment.

'Ranjubaba,' said Jose, his teeth chattering a little as he spoke, 'where's the r-river?'

'The river is f-f-frozen. That *is* the river,' he replied, pointing to the glacier.

'The source? That's the s-source? You mean we've found it?' said Jose, thinking this cannot be the Eternal Spring, surely. Eternal winter, more like.

'Chill-children, ice flows too. You must journey to where the glacier begins.'

'B-but...that's... I mean, how are we...?' Jose looked up towards the snow-shrouded peaks that loomed in front of them and his heart sank. He was just so tired.

Ranjubaba had arranged himself in a lotus position and was sitting, eyes closed, in order to 'channel his prana' as he put it. The children sat close by as he breathed rapidly through one nostril, then the other, puffing like a steam engine. It sounded like someone sawing through a log. His moustache and beard were decorated with icicles and his hair looked even more like a mountainscape, topped with snowy peaks.

The children watched him for a while in silence.

Then he appeared to give up.

'It's no g-g-good,' he announced. 'My k-k-kundalini refuses to rise. In f-f-fact,' he lifted up his haunches and rubbed his bottom ruefully, 'I think it may be f-f-frozen to a p-p-popsicle.'

'We have to keep moving,' said Jose (rather reluctantly, for although it was good to keep warm, his legs were aching terribly and he wanted nothing more than to sit down for a while at least, and gather his strength).

Mishi agreed. 'We can't just stand here,' she said, 'we have to carry on.'

'Follow the glacier,' said Ranjubaba. 'You must c-c-continue to go against the f-flow.'

'Wait. You mean,' said Jose, 'aren't you coming with us?'

Ranjubaba shook his head and his dreadlocks wobbled, sending a flurry of snow down onto his bare shoulders.

'I'm afraid I cannot,' he said slowly. 'I must return to my c-cave. I have to look after my p-plants, my herbs. It is,' he spread his hands in a resigned gesture, 'it is my *d-d-dharma*.'

'But...' Jose suddenly realised how much he liked having a grown-up with them, even if said grown-up was half-naked, had mad hair, and kept talking about cows and flowers and prana and popsicles. In fact, he had grown rather fond of this strange little man, and the prospect of him and Mishi carrying on, on their own, into this vast icy land filled him with cold dread.

Ranjubaba got to his feet. He embraced the children in turn, his eyes wet, though whether from sadness or the effect of the wind, they couldn't tell.

'G-g-goodbye, my children,' he said. 'I must turn b-back now. B-blessings upon you. Thank you. I feel that my Guruji is back: here,' and he put his hand over his heart, 'and for that I shall be eternally g-grateful. But our paths must diverge. You have your qu-quest, and I have m-mine. Insh'allah, we shall m-m-meet again.'

And then he turned and started back down the mountain. The children stood in the meagre shelter of the rocks and watched until the little bare-bodied figure was swallowed up in the swirling white wilderness and was lost to sight.

Mishi and Jose trudged slowly through the snow and ice, wrapped in their own thoughts. Jose was thinking that it was all very well for Perveen to say 'follow the river', when no one had thought to mention that it would turn into a bloomin' great glacier. Mishi was mostly hoping that they wouldn't bump into another huge, hairy – possibly hungry – notyeti.

The wind had died down, but it was still snowing heavily. Soft flakes landed on their hair and shoulders, and lay thickly on the ground, muffling all sound, filling in their footprints behind them.

'I wonder if we'll ever make it back to school?' said Jose – more to himself than anything.

'School?' said Mishi. The word made her think of somewhere safe, somewhere warm – somewhere she belonged. But Gravepyres itself – the buildings, the teachers, the hallways and corridors had all receded, swallowed up in her mind by the same swirling white haze that enveloped the land around them.

They had no idea how far they had come, or how far they still had to go. Everything beyond them and everything behind them was hidden. The sky above and the ground beneath were one blurred mass of shifting shapes, grey and white and almost indistinguishable from each other. There was just Jose and Mishi, the silence and the snow.

The snow, now up to their knees, showed no signs of stopping. Each step was agony as Jose hauled one foot out of the snow and placed the next one down, sinking down and struggling out, one foot after the other. Time had no meaning, distance even less. After who knew how long, or how far, Jose felt himself stagger and fall, and – with a brief flicker of relief that it was all over – lay unmoving. Mishi stumbled towards him and tried to lift the dead weight of his body. But it was no use. He was too heavy, and she was too small. And too tired. So very, very tired. She lay down beside him, curled up, and knew no more.

When Jose came to, he felt himself swaying and rocking, far above the ground. His eyes flickered open – and then he quickly shut them tight.

The thing that was carrying him was hairy and huge.

The notyeti was ploughing through the deep snow like a cargo ship through a stormy sea, snow swirling in spumes of white, with Jose tucked firmly under one arm. He registered a momentary surge of blinding panic and nausea – where was Mishi? Had the notyeti eaten her up? But then he peered across and saw that the creature was carrying a small bundle tucked under its other hairy arm, and breathed a sigh of relief.

Then he heard a snuffly hoot and looked up. The baby notyeti was perched on its mother's shoulder, wearing a white cap of snow and peeking down at him like a sailor looking over the side of a boat. When it saw that Jose was awake, it hooted excitedly. And Jose couldn't help but smile: he was glad to see it. Perhaps it was the sheer relief of being out of the biting wind, snuggled against the creature's warm furry body, or perhaps it was the effect of the heady scent – laden with procrastin, a hormone unique to notyetis – that enveloped him in a glorious blanket of forgetfulness, but Jose gave up any idea of struggle and fell into a sort of trance, letting himself be carried along, not worrying about the past or the future. Gravepyres seemed like a distant memory, his past life a vague dream. There was nothing but the gentle rocking of his body with each giant step as the ground flew by beneath them and Jose surrendered gratefully to the beckoning tug of sleep.

The notyeti strode through the blizzard, unconcerned, driven on by some deep instinct. The two young cubs she had come across, almost entirely covered by snow and frozen to the marrow, had helped her own baby escape from that nasty tangled contraption. They seemed like newborns, not even old enough to have grown proper fur. So the notyeti had scooped them up, light as feathers, and tucked one under each arm. She grunted and carried on, mile after mile, large and implacable, feeling neither tiredness nor cold: a creature of the mountains in the mountains, as calm and powerful as a humpback whale swimming through the ocean deep.

Jose was in the middle of a warm and happy dream when he suddenly realised he couldn't breathe. He struggled and thrashed, and then gasped awake. Mishi was hunkered over him, pinching his nose shut. As soon as she saw he was awake, she signalled to him with wide, terrified eyes, keeping a firm grip on his nose with one hand and putting the fingers of her other hand to her lips. 'Breathe through your mouth,' she said in an urgent whisper. Then she took a strip of cloth that she had torn from the bottom of her tunic and tied it swiftly around his face, so that it looked like a robber's mask. Jose followed her eyes to the mouth of the cave where the notyeti was hunkered down, busily grooming her baby, searching through its hair with long, leathery black fingers.

Outside, the wind swept past, moaning and howling. There was no way out, their escape route blocked by the enormous beast. Inside the cavern lay several great heaps of wood, twigs and leaves and entire branches of pine that looked like they'd been ripped bodily from the tree. Padded with armfuls of dried moss, they looked like vast nests – and so they were, for the cave was the lair of the notyetis and had been for countless generations. On the ground around them, Jose realised with horror that what he had taken to be bits of dried wood and branches were in fact whitened bones, chewed and gnawed at the ends.

As silently as they could, Mishi and Jose got on to all fours and crawled towards the back of the cave. Then they froze at the sound of a deep gruffling growl behind them. Mishi grabbed the nearest weapon – a long, knobbly shinbone of some long-deceased animal – and clutched it to her chest. Just then the baby notyeti, who had clearly had enough of being groomed and had clambered on to its mother's head, sank its sharp little teeth into her leathery ear. The mother, losing patience, plucked it up and held it upside down by one foot in front of her, where it swung happily, hooting. She cuffed the baby none too gently round the ear, settled it back firmly in her lap and continued grooming, ignoring its muffled bleats of protest.

Jose, still looking like a bandit with his improvised mask, and Mishi, still clutching her bone club, continued on all fours towards the back of the cave. After a while, they came to an opening in the rock. It was too low to stand up in, but also too small for the notyeti to get through, so they wordlessly made their way into it, Jose in front, and Mishi behind.

Crawling along in the darkness, painfully conscious of the low ceiling of rock just above his head, Jose fought down a feeling of claustrophobia. At any moment they could come to a dead end, and if they did, Mishi would have to crawl backwards and so would he, all the way back to the cave – there was no room to even turn around. Jose felt the ground sloping down as they inched their way forward into the heart of the mountain.

After what felt like hours, Jose sensed something different about the air. He stopped abruptly, and Mishi bumped into his bottom. 'Shhh, hang on,' he said, and lifted one hand up. Instead of the roof of the tunnel, his hand met nothing. Jose tentatively got to his feet. 'We can stand up here,' he said.

Mishi crawled along to where he stood and got to her feet too, and looked around. With their eyes adjusted to the darkness, they could now make out a faint glittering light ahead.

'You can take this off now, I think,' said Mishi. So Jose pushed the facemask down around his neck where it hung like a bandana. He took an experimental sniff.

'Are you okay?' said Mishi.

Jose checked in on himself. No wooziness, no sudden urge to collect flowers or have a little nap. 'Yes,' he said.

'Good. Maybe the smell can't get this far.' Mishi had tucked her bone-club into the belt at her waist, where it hung like a white sword on a small and rather unconvincing knight.

'There must be another way out,' said Jose. 'Look.'

He pointed ahead to where the tunnel branched into two. The opening to the left was slightly larger and had a thin stream of water flowing along the bottom. They had no idea really which one to choose, but since they had been 'following the river' for so long, they decided to continue doing just that.

Where the water flowed over it, the rock was smooth and slippery as soap. The children steadied themselves on the cavern walls with their hands, and picked their way along the side, trying to keep their feet dry.

After a little while they emerged into a wide underground cavern. The roof was a jagged mass of spikes – like an inverted mountain range, each spike tapering down to a wickedly sharp point. The floor of the cavern was a forest of stalagmites, thousands of them. Some were only as high as Mishi's knees, but others towered over them, as big as the trunks of full-grown trees. Here and there crystals of calcite bloomed like flowers of ice. The whole place was suffused with a soft glow, glistening with the ancient light of mineral phosphorescence.

'Look. Over there,' said Mishi, pointing to the far side of the cavern where the rocks rose to form a kind of shallow basin. Water overflowed its smooth curved sides in a steady stream, flowing down the rock and gathering in a clear, sparkling pool at the bottom, and then snaking its way through the labyrinth of stalagmites. The water emitted a soft blue radiance that flickered and sparkled on the overhang above, as though it were filled with pale fire. Jose stood on tiptoe, excitement seeming to lift him up until his very hair tingled.

'That's it,' he whispered, his eyes blazing. 'That's it, Mishi. We've found it. The Eternal Spring.'

The two children just stood for a while, transfixed, unable to move. Then Jose seemed to recollect why they were here in the first place. 'The seed,' he said, breaking the spell. 'We have to find the seed. It must be here somewhere.'

'Oh, yes,' said Mishi. 'Right.' They looked around and then split up to search.

They picked their way across the floor of the cave through the towering cones of rock, scanning the ground. Once, Jose found what looked like a white or whitish pebble, but it wasn't perfectly round, and when he picked it up to examine it, it turned out to be just an ordinary stone. He flung it down. The children made their way slowly around the whole chamber, and finally met again in the middle, Jose on one side of the stream, Mishi on the other.

'Anything?' he said, his voice echoing across. Mishi just shrugged and held out her empty hands.

'Okay,' he said. 'You try this side, and I'll try over there.'

Jose jumped across the water and continued to search. Mishi watched him for a while, and then sat down at the water's edge where the lip of the basin formed a little waterfall. She put her fingers into the icy stream and watched as the water played through her fingers, twisting this way and that. Then she hauled herself up to the side and stared into the pool. The bottom was covered with tiny multicoloured pebbles: coral and turquoise, rose quartz and aquamarine. It was so beautiful and so clear.

Mishi lay down on her front and gazed down. Then she plunged her face into the water and opened her eyes.

And that's when everything came back.

Memories came bubbling up, flooding her mind, threatening to sweep her away. She remembered lying on a hard stone floor as a baby and crying in loss and bewilderment. She remembered an old man with a silver scythe and eyes like burning coals wrapping her into the velvet folds of his cloak and carrying her inside, murmuring words that soothed her and stopped the tears. She remembered the first word to issue from her mouth – not 'mama' or 'baba' or 'papa' but 'Ya-ma' – two syllables spelling out the word for comfort and love. With a stab of longing, she remembered Gravepyres – its wooden carvings, corridors and courtyard, its towers of stone and quaint upturned tiled roofs – her home, the only one she had ever known. A place full of children, children who came and went, endlessly, endlessly. Faces floated before her, each one different from the next, vivid and unique: dark-haired, light-skinned, with curly mops or straight hair, ragged or neat, girls, boys, shy, mischievous, plump, thin, freckled, tanned, eyes brown or blue or green, happy faces, sad ones. Leo, Zainab and Ali; Xi, Janet, Piotr, Aleksandr and Sian; Imani, Maha, Willow, Rosie and Aaryan: Jennifer and Ademar and Thadeo, Alan, Ishan, Jyoti... So many names, so many children. And Professor Styx's kindly voice saying, 'You'll look after them, won't you, Mishi?' And then she remembered how each new friend, one after the other, had left her, left her quite alone... and how – until this very second – she had forgotten them all.

She pushed herself back out of the pool. Water dripped from her eyelashes, ran down her cheeks and fell in glittering droplets. How could she have forgotten? How? She sat there staring at her own reflection: the face of a familiar stranger, with eyes as old as the universe.

Jose meanwhile, having circled the cave twice and come back empty-handed, was ready to admit defeat. He came over and plonked himself down next to her.

'You're all wet,' he said. 'Why are you wet?' And then he frowned at her. 'You were looking, weren't you? You do remember what we're supposed to be looking *for*?'

'I remember everything,' she said simply.

'Oh. Good,' said Jose, his mind elsewhere. And then he went on, running his hands dejectedly through his hair. 'I just don't understand. It *has* to be here somewhere...'

Mishi looked at him. Jose with his mop of unruly hair. Jose with his wonky front tooth. Jose, who always looked so lost in class, who tried so hard, who would bite his lower lip when he was trying to figure something out – like he was just now. Jose with the sad eyes, who missed his family so much. Jose: her friend. He looked so forlorn, sitting there with his head in his hands. Mishi put a hand on his shoulder.

'It's hopeless,' he said. 'We've looked everywhere. What are we supposed to do now? I mean, how are we ever going to find...'

'Wait,' said Mishi suddenly. 'What did you just say?'

'What? I said, it's hopeless. We've searched...'

'Looking... you said "looking". Maybe we *shouldn't* look. Maybe that's the problem.'

Jose looked at her quizzically.

'I mean, what if we do Seeing? You know, like in Dr Chiplunker's class.'

'That's not...' started Jose, 'I mean, I can't...'

'Try,' said Mishi.

And so he did.

Clearing his mind of thought and preconceptions, he viewed the cave as though from far away, as though there was a great distance between where he was looking from and the surface of his eye. Each time he registered a word – 'rock,' 'green', 'crystal', 'tower', 'teeth', 'water' – he tried to let it go, and instead concentrated on the pattern of dark and light. He began to let go of the idea of depth: there was no 'near' and 'far', just the play of form and shape revealing itself before his steady gaze. Then, after a long while, like someone flipping a switch, like one of those multi-coloured paintings that suddenly clicks into a 3D landscape in front of your eyes, he Saw.

Scattered on the ground, lodged into crannies in the wall, balanced on top of stalagmites, dangling from the tips of stalactites – hundreds of pearly seeds, hidden in plain sight, just waiting to be noticed.

He gave a little cry and jumped down from the ledge. He ran about gathering seeds and stuffing them into his pockets. Mishi smiled to herself as she opposite of fine! What if going back meant she started to forget again? Up here in the mountains, everything was so shiningly clear. What if, when they got back to Gravepyres, she couldn't remember the children – Xanthe and Keitaro and Debashree and all the rest? She would rather go back to the lair of the notyetis than forget them all over again... She felt like she was losing her mind.

Jose was looking at her, nonplussed. He had long since given up trying to figure out Mishi and her motivations.

'Look,' he said, exasperated, '*you* can stay here if you want to: I'm going back.' And with that, he started down the mountain.

Mishi watched him go, paralysed with indecision.

'You can't... you can't leave me!' she finally burst out. Her voice echoed around the mountains.

'Well, come *on* then!' he shouted back.

Mishi stood for a moment, rooted to the spot. She clenched her fists and made a vow: she would never forget them again, never, ever. Then, a look of utter determination on her face she slithered down to join him.

It was slow going. With every step they sank up to their shins in the powdery snow and had to haul themselves out. They slipped and trudged and waded along until Mishi spotted a lone pine tree and made her way towards it. A piece of bark had splintered off

watched him. Finally, he ran back to her. He took a single seed from his pocket and placed it in the palm of her hand. It lay just where her heart-line and head-line met at the line of fate, shining softly like a tiny full moon.

'Beautiful,' she said, and handed it back to him.

Jose closed his hand around the seed, and sent up a prayer of utter thankfulness. The expression in Mishi's eyes was quite different from her usual dreamy, faraway look as she gazed up at her friend's radiant face.

With his pockets bulging with seeds, Jose couldn't wait to get back down the mountain.

'We can't go the way we came,' said Mishi. She didn't want to risk a close encounter of the notyeti kind any time soon. Jose agreed.

'What about up there?' he said, pointing.

On the far side of the cave, a series of twisting rocks poked up through a slither of scree. At the top was a disc – almost like a porthole – glazed with mottled glass. The two children clambered up towards it, and when they reached it they realised that it was glazed, not with glass but with compacted snow. Jose pushed against it, but it was frozen solid.

Then Mishi took the bone from her belt and brandished it above her head. She bashed at the opening and managed to dislodge a shower of ice chips. Balancing on a narrow ledge, Jose took over battering the club-like end of the bone against the

ice, until finally, with one great whack, a chun_ ice dislodged and fell with a clatter to the ca_ floor. Jose poked the club upwards and the top j_ disappeared.

'It's soft,' said Jose excitedly. 'Snow!'

He hacked and poked until the small coin_ bright blue sky grew and widened, and he was ab_ to get first an arm, then his head, then his whol_ body through. He lay on the snow and reached down_ through the ice for Mishi. She grabbed his hands and he heaved backwards, dragging her out of the icy hole like an Eskimo landing a seal.

The world outside was a white wonderland.

The sky was blue as a periwinkle and the snow lay like a carpet of crushed diamonds, sparkling in every direction. There was no sign of the notyetis.

'Right,' said Jose, taking a deep breath of cold air, 'let's get going.'

'Do we have to?' said Mishi.

Jose looked at her like she'd gone completely mad. 'Well, of course we have to,' he exclaimed. 'Look at all these seeds! Now I've got these, I'm sure I'll be able to make it through the lake – with or without the vultures' help. I *know* I can get home now. Things will go back to how they are supposed to be and everything's going to be fine!'

But it's not, thought Mishi desperately. If everything goes back to how it was, that's the exact and fallen to the ground. She lifted up one end and brushed away the snow. 'How about this?'

Jose and Mishi heaved the hunk of bark to the top of the glacier. Mishi sat in front and Jose hooked his legs on either side of her, and they pushed off, zooming down the slope. The snow was coated with a sparkling layer of hard frost, and the glacier looked like a huge silver slide in a giant's playground. Mishi's shawl streamed out behind her, flapping in Jose's face, and his eyes stung with cold as they sailed down the mountain. It took all their concentration to keep their balance, and it was so exhilarating to be finally out in the clean, fresh air that it was impossible to worry or even think as the world rushed by them in a blur.

The small technical hitch they soon discovered – that there was no way either to steer or to brake – was solved for them by a very large bank of snow. They ended their wild ride in a crumpled, giggling heap.

'Wooo!' said Mishi, dusting herself down. 'That was fun!'

Their bark-sleigh had delivered them to the bottom of the glacier. In the distance they could see the river winding its way down towards the black spill of the reservoir far below.

Every so often, Jose would put his hand in his pocket to make sure the seeds were safe and sound. They had done it! They would be back at school in no time! It was all going to be okay.

But further down the mountain, something else was afoot. Sinister figures crept through the forest. Men in black overalls and heavy boots, armed with guns, made their way silently towards a clearing in the trees. At a signal from their leader, they dropped down and covered their faces with snouted masks. They had learned their lesson about the effects of the notyeti's scent, and this time they were taking no chances. They lay in wait, guns at the ready. Suddenly, a notyeti broke into the glade – a huge foot came down on the tripwire – the massive net fell – and with a howl and a roar, the poor creature flailed and struggled as dart after dart was fired into her thick fur until she finally fell senseless to the forest floor.

The children reached the same clearing several hours later. They saw the broken branches and trampled ground, the mud churned up by heavy tyre-treads. 'What...?' started Jose, but before he could finish, he was nearly knocked off his feet by a small furry creature that launched itself into his arms, hooting madly. The baby notyeti wrapped its arms around his neck, and Jose could feel its little body trembling. 'Hello, you,' he said. 'Where's your mummy, then?'

The baby climbed down from his shoulders and scampered across to the far edge of the clearing where the tyre tracks led off down the mountainside. 'I'll bet it's those nasty men from the Dam,' muttered Mishi. 'Damming everything. Well, dam *them*.'

They set off through the trees, the baby clinging to Jose like a small furry rucksack. By the time they reached the forest near the construction site, it was almost dark. In the half-light, they could make out where the tracks had churned up the mud around the gate. The children stayed in the shadows, on the other side of the perimeter fence, and the baby notyeti clambered down from Jose's back.

On the other side of the wire, floodlights lit the scene like a stage set. Men swarmed around a huge stainless steel machine, shouting to each other and gesticulating. At one end of the machine was a great grey funnel that led down into a round container that looked like an enormous concrete mixer. There was a control panel on one side bristling with levers, dials and switches. Stencilled on the side of the machine were the words:

PLASTICATION UNIT

WARNING! HARD HAT ZONE

YOUR SAFETY, OUR PRIORITY

The machine squatted silently, like some malevolent metal toad, its mouth open to the sky.

Then there was a roar of engines and a sudden flurry of activity as a crane clanked to life. A man on the ground was waving up at the crane operator to lower a huge hook into the clearing. Several men swung the hook over and attached it to a large metal crate. The first man signalled again, the cable was winched up, and the crate swung slowly across the yard towards the machine. The hairs on the back of Jose's neck stood up as he heard the unmistakable hoots and grunts of the notyeti, and the crate itself swung wildly on the hook as the creature inside banged against the sides, desperate to get out.

And it wasn't just the children who heard the notyeti. Jose suddenly grabbed Mishi's arm and pointed, horrified, at the little notyeti who had set off on her hind legs at a tottering run, straight into the glare of the floodlights and towards the platform where the crate had finally come to rest alongside three or four others.

'Come ba...' Mishi's yell was cut short by Jose's hand clamped over her mouth. He put his finger to his lips.

He beckoned to her, and Mishi followed him around the edge of the trees, just beyond the circle of light. They got as close to the Plastication Unit as possible, scanning the scene frantically, but couldn't see the baby notyeti anywhere.

'What are we going to do?' hissed Mishi.

'I don't know, I don't know, I don't know,' muttered Jose, biting his lip.

'Jose! Look!' Mishi pointed to a gap in the fence where the wires didn't quite reach the ground, and before he could stop her, she was running towards it and wriggling her way through to the other side. Jose watched in horror as she crept along, edging her way closer to what he now saw was a toolbox, lying forgotten to one side of the Plastication Unit. He had no idea what she was planning to do – but as long as the men didn't turn around, she might just...

'*Oi!*'

One of the men had seen her. She started to run back towards Jose, but the man caught her easily, grabbing her roughly by the shoulders. Jose watched, helpless, as she was dragged, kicking and yelling, across the floodlit yard.

The man pushed Mishi towards a building where another construction worker was standing. The second man tilted back his yellow hardhat and looked down at her with narrowed eyes.

'Well, well. What 'ave we got 'ere?'

'Let me go!' snarled Mishi, struggling.

'I dunno. Found it lurkin' near the plasticator,' said the first man.

'A spy, I reckon,' said the other. He caught hold of Mishi's chin and twisted her face this way and that. 'A sneakin' 'orrid little spy.'

'Am not!' cried Mishi and kicked him in the shin.

'Ow! Right, yer bloomin' little sneak. We'll see what the Boss 'as to say about that.' And they frogmarched her inside.

The building itself was not very much more than a prefabricated hut. The first room was a rather functional office, with printers, a water dispenser, a few office chairs and two desks facing each other. The men marched Mishi straight through the room, to a door at the end, which was marked 'Dexter J. Tannenbaum: Director and Chief Executionary Officer'.

They knocked and the first man opened the door.

Sitting behind a large desk was a man in a dark grey suit and tie. On the desk were a sleek silver laptop computer, a bowl of fruit and a half-finished Lego model of a spaceship.

'Did I say "enter"? Did I?' he said crossly, sweeping bits of Lego into a drawer.

'Uh, sorry, sah,' said the first man, backing out a bit. 'May we…enter?'

'Enter,' said Mr Tannenbaum, with a grand wave of his hand.

'Thank you, sah,' said the man, and pushed Mishi forward.

Dexter J. Tannenbaum was incredibly handsome. His features were almost mathematically symmetrical. His nose was straight and neat, his eyebrows dark and commanding, his eyes a beguiling shade of hazel. His teeth gleamed, perfectly straight and even. He looked like a movie star – no, actually, he looked like someone had cherry-picked all the most attractive features of all the movie stars there had ever been and sort of poured them all into this one impossibly divine package. He ran his fingers through his sleek coif of dark brown hair and raised one eyebrow.

'And what have we here?' he purred.

'It's a spy, sah,' said the second man. 'We captured it.'

'*I* captured...' muttered his mate, but the other man ignored him and carried on, '...sneakin' around the fence it was.'

'It? Really guys? *It?*' said Tannenbaum.

The men shuffled their feet a bit.

'This is not an "it",' the director went on. 'This is a "she".'

'But it's... I mean *she*'s a spy, sah. A nasty, sneaky little spy.'

'I see,' said Tannenbaum. He stood up and came to the front of the desk. He leant back against it, half-sitting, and folded his hands in his lap, regarding Mishi with those melty hazelnut eyes. 'And what do you have to say to that?'

'I'm not a *spy*,' said Mishi, hotly, 'I wasn't *sneaking*. I wasn't DOING anything. I was just looking. There's no law against that!'

'Well, as a matter of fact,' said Tannenbaum, going to the shelf behind his desk and taking down a huge leather-bound book with *Irrefutable Laws of Time, Volume One* in gold letters down the spine, '...there is.' He found a page and ran his finger down it, muttering. 'Damning evidence, Article 4950: "persons

168

known or unknown"... "within, on, around or in the vicinity..." yada, yada, yada... yup, here it is: Clause 58, para C, "shall be detained for a minimum of 108 mahayugs, otherwise known as All Eternity. This is a non-bailable offence."'

'You can't keep me here for all eternity!' cried Mishi.

'Oh, but honey,' smiled the director, showing all his perfect teeth, 'we so totally *can.*'

'YOU...you... you captured the notyeti! *That's* an nonblabble fence, I bet. If you hurt it...'

'Hurt it?' The director raised his hand, a pained expression on his angelic face. 'Why would we wanna hurt it? We're going to *fix* it.'

'But it's not *broken!*' Mishi shouted.

Mr Tannenbaum smiled his dazzling smile. Then he turned to the workmen. 'Okay guys, you can go. I'll take it from here.'

When they had gone, he pulled out a chair. 'We got off on the wrong foot, uh...'

'Mishi,' said Mishi.

'... Mishi. Let's start over. I'm Dexter J. Tannenbaum – you can call me Dexter – and I'm the director of this state-of-the-art, ahead-of-its-time facility that you were, ah, not sneaking around.'

Mishi started to protest.

'Hey, hey,' he said, 'I'm sure you had your reasons, okay? Simmer down.' He reached for the fruit bowl. 'Have a bañana.'

'I don't want a ban…yana,' said Mishi crossly. 'I don't want anything.'

'Uh-huh,' nodded the director, peeling himself one. 'You sure about that?'

'You seem like a smart young lady,' he carried on. 'Sit down, why don't ya, and I'll fill you in.'

Mishi perched on the edge of one of the chairs and waited.

'Plasticorp,' began the director, 'the biggest and most powerful organisation the world has ever known. Founded by this guy here,' and here he looked up at the framed photograph behind his desk, 'Godfrey Gilgamesh the Third.' The photo showed an imposing man – silver-haired, with penetrating eyes and a nose as sharp and curved as an eagle's beak. He stood at a slight angle to the camera, looking down, his mouth set in a grim line.

'GG was a visionary,' the director went on, warming to his theme, 'a leader. He was The Man. With a Plan. He dared to dream. To dream of a day – the glorious day – of the death of Death.'

'The death of Death?' said Mishi, puzzled.

'Yup, you said it. Imagine: no more pain, no more loss, no more old age… Pretty good, huh?'

'But… but that's impossible,' said Mishi.

'Nothing was impossible for GG,' said the director, picking another bañana from the bowl and handing it to Mishi. 'Everyone wanted a piece of his research.

Others were wasting their time on anti-ageing cream, ziplock, Tupperware! Organ transplants, cryogenic freezing – that was child's play. GG had bigger ideas, he was playing the long game, understand? And that's when he finally invented... braiding.'

'Braiding?' said Mishi. 'Like pigtails?'

'Y... no. Braiding is... basically you take living DNA, the fundamental building block of life, right? An organism's genetic code. And you twist it together with plastic polymers.' He twined his long fingers together. 'Kinda like plaits, yes, but on a, like, micro-level. And that is what this Dam is all about. Taking the DNA of every known species, braiding it with the plastic polymers and extruding them into building blocks that are impervious to Time itself.'

'What do you mean, "every known species"?'

'Aardvark to zebu, baby. Aardvark to zebu.' The director tossed his bañana skin into the bin. 'There was only one species we didn't have – the missing link, you might say.'

Light dawned on Mishi's face. 'The notyeti.'

'Bingo.' He shot her with his forefinger. 'We managed to trap a cub, but that got away. Somehow. But this is so much better: a fully grown female.'

'But... Mister Tannenbaum,' ('Dexter, *please*,') 'I still don't understand. How is that supposed to *fix* anything?'

'Think about it. No Time, no decay. No decay, no death. Perpetual pristine perfection. *Mortem ad mortem*, as GG used to say. Eternal life, honey. It's all good.'

Mishi's mind was racing. She really didn't want to go back to Gravepyres. After everything that had happened, the idea of going back to 'normal life' (or normal death, to be precise) had no appeal. If she couldn't stay in the mountains, and she couldn't go back to the school – maybe this was the solution. Perpetual pristine perfection, permanently half way between the two. Mr Tannenbaum seemed really nice. She took in his tanned skin, his flawlessly perfect features, and wondered...

'Can they do it to people?'

'Plastication? Sure,' said Dexter. 'Feel.' And he leaned forward, and offered her his cheek.

She stroked the side of his face. 'Ooooh. Smooooth,' she said.

'What'd I tell ya? It's all good, Mishi honey. One little prick,' he mimed an injection, 'and *voilà!* It's a whole new You.'

Seeing the look on her face, Tannenbaum smoothed down his tie, stood up and held out his hand. 'Listen,' he said, 'we're a little behind schedule here. Once we get the last few blocks in place, we'll do you. I promise – you won't feel a thing.'

While all this was going on, Jose was outside the fence, in the darkness at the edge of the forest, hopping from foot to foot in an agony of indecision. He had seen Mishi being captured and taken into the building, and then nothing had happened for an ominously long time. Should he go after her? But what if they captured him too? And what if they'd done something awful to Mishi? What would he do then? But what if he didn't do anything? But what *could* he do? Jose knew from reading lots of adventure stories that usually at this point, the hero suddenly remembers something that had been given to him earlier on – like a vial of potion, or a magic bugle or something – with stern instructions to only use it 'in the hour of need'. Well, if this didn't count as an 'hour of need', he didn't know what would! He shoved his hands in his pockets and pulled out a fistful of seeds. Yessssssss!

But... what was he supposed to do with them? Chuck them at one of the workmen? He looked at them for a moment, glowing like beads of moonstone in his hand. Beautiful... and utterly, utterly useless! He rummaged some more – and came up with a pencil stub and some bits of fluff.

The questions started up again in ever more frantic circles, and he was back to 'should he/shouldn't he go after her' for about the fiftieth time, when the door of the Plasticorp building opened and out came two figures – a tall man and a small girl.

Jose nearly cried out in relief. She was okay!

The two figures headed towards the Plastication Unit.

The man said something to one of the workers, who nodded and then walked towards the plasticator and twiddled some buttons on the control panel. He flipped a lever and, with a sickening roar and a belch of black smoke, the machine lurched to life.

Jose watched, horrified, as the crane lifted up the first of the crates to the top of the funnel, and a mechanical arm swung over and tipped the whole thing up, cascading the contents – which yowled and scrambled and scratched and leapt – into its gaping maw. There was a crunching, slicing, grinding sound from the belly of the slowly rotating machine – then there was a hideous screech like nails on a blackboard, and a dull thud as a rectangular block dropped onto the conveyor belt at the other end. All the poor animals that had been fed into the top had been completely and utterly plasticated. Jose felt sick.

He couldn't understand why Mishi wasn't doing anything. She was just standing there, watching the horror unfold, an expression of mild interest on her face.

He knew he had to do something – but what? Then he spotted a dark shape on the ground: the toolbox! Without a second thought, he scrambled under the wire and ran towards it. He wrenched it open and grabbed whatever he could lay his hands on. With all the noise and the lights, none of the men operating the machinery noticed the small boy sprinting around to the back. They were busy fixing the hook to the next crate.

The crate was lifted into the sky and swung back and forth as the creature (or creatures) inside scrambled and howled.

There was no time to lose. Jose stared up at the machine that towered high above him, juddering and chuntering as though it was hungry for more, and concentrated all his years of cricket practice into this one throw. He lobbed the spanner in a high arc and watched as it hung for a second, glittering, and then plunged into the funnel. *Yes!* A perfect shot! The machine screeched, growled and sputtered to a halt.

'What the...' Tannenbaum threw up his hands.

'Dammit! I thought you guys had fixed this thing.' He strode off to consult with the technicians.

This was Jose's chance. He sneaked up behind Mishi and grabbed her hand. 'Come on,' he whispered urgently.

'Oh hallo,' said Mishi. 'What are you doing here?'

'Er, rescuing you?'

She shrugged. 'It's okay, ackcherly. I'm fine.'

'What? What d'you...? Fine?' Jose spluttered incoherently.

'Well yes, I will be anyway,' Mishi insisted. 'Mister Tannenbaum – Dexter – said that I could be plasticated too.'

'Are you *out of your mind*?' hissed Jose, looking up at the giant funnel. 'You *want* to go in that thing?'

'Not like that,' she explained patiently. 'Just a little injection. A little DNA braiding and *voilà!* It doesn't even hurt. Dexter said so.'

'I'm not arguing with you,' Jose said, trying to pull her away.

'Yes, you are. You're all angry.'

'Mishi! What's wrong with you??' Any minute now, the men would be back. They were seriously running out of time. Jose grabbed her by the shoulders. 'You have to come with me *right now*,' he said fiercely. 'If you don't, I'll... I'll never forgive you.'

Jose knew in his heart of hearts that he would never have got this far without her, and the thought of losing her – of carrying on alone – was too much to bear. 'I need you,' he said.

Mishi looked down, to hide the anguish on her face. If only he had stopped at forgiving, she thought to herself. If only he'd stopped there. Jose didn't understand – would never understand – that she had been given a chance at a different kind of life, or rather, a different kind of death. An existence with no rough edges, no heartbreak, no decay, no loss – pristine perfection forever – and now she was watching it slip away on a little raft made of three small words. She was needed, and that was enough. She heaved her small shoulders up and down, and the look in her eyes held a kind of resigned bravery, like someone about to jump out of a plane trusting to someone else's parachute.

'Well, why didn't you say so?' she said, grabbing his hand.

And with that, the two children ran helter-skelter for the forest.

They had just made it to the edge of the trees when a shout went up.

'The spy! She's gone!'

The children heard the director's voice, harsh and loud, all trace of silvery smoothness gone. 'Goddammit! Get after her – she can't have got far. We gotta fix her.'

From the tops of the watchtowers, searchlights

strafed the forest, and the children ran for their lives through bars of light and dark, in a desperate scramble to get away. They squeezed through the hole in the wire; the workmen had to backtrack to the main gate. That gave them a good head-start, but the men were gaining on them fast.

'Mishi,' Jose half-panted, half-moaned, as they crashed through the trees, 'I can't... what are we going to do?'

'Quick!' cried Mishi. 'Up here.' She grabbed a low branch and swung herself up into a tree. Jose scrambled up behind her and they hid amongst the dense foliage.

And not a moment too soon. The men who had been chasing them came to a halt right below the tree where they were hiding.

'Where'd she go?' said one.

'Dunno,' said the other gruffly. 'Wild bloomin' goose chase if you ask me. She could be 'arf way down the valley by now.'

'I toldja we should've just bunged 'er in the plasticator when we 'ad a chance.'

'Yeah, well, we're not gonna get much further in this dark,' said the first man. 'May as well wait it out 'ere for a bit.'

'Nah, let's go back. I 'ate this forest. They reckon there's all sorts up 'ere: ghosts, churails... brrr. Gives me the creeps it does.'

'Everyfing gives you the creeps, yer great ninny. Any'ow, we can't go back now, Boss'll give us 'ell. We'll tell 'im we went as far as the ridge, okay?' The man eased off his hat and settled down on the ground, leaning against the tree trunk.

The children were trapped. The men only had to look up and they would see them. They couldn't make a sound… and, of course, as soon as he thought that, Jose had the terrible, tickling, urgent desire to sneeze.

He scrunched up his face, held his nose and squeezed his eyes shut. Then he opened his eyes – and nearly fell out of the tree. There were TWO pairs of eyes staring back! Squatting on a branch near Mishi, bony knees up about his ears, looking like a large, mad-haired owl, was Ranjubaba. He put his hands together in a silent 'namaste' and unslung a cloth bag from his shoulder.

From inside, he took out another, smaller bag and carefully, without rustling a leaf or snapping a twig, shook it out gently. A soft snowfall of fluffy seed heads whirled slowly down on the men sitting below, falling on their cheeks and down the backs of their collars. Nothing happened for a while, and then one started to scratch. Then the other. Then they both jumped up, itching and scratching for all they were worth.

'I'm getting bitten!'

'You sat us on an anthill, ya berk.'

They hopped up and down in a kind of mad squirmy breakdance.

Ranjubaba looked at the children and grinned. Then he dug into his bag again. He flung a fistful of pods that burst on impact, sending hard black seeds pinging around like gunshot. 'Puffapods!' whispered Ranjubaba to Mishi delightedly.

'Wass that? 'Oo's there? Ow! Someone's shootin' us!'

'I toldja it was haunted!'

That gave Jose an idea. He cupped his hands to his mouth and let out a low 'oooooo'. Mishi immediately caught on. She bugged out her eyes and sagged her mouth, and let out the most mournful, haunting, marrowbone-chilling 'woooooo' she could possibly muster. '*Churaaaaiiiiiils!*' they shrieked, and took off, crashing through the trees as fast as their legs could carry them.

Mishi and Jose climbed carefully down to the ground. When Ranjubaba jumped down nimbly and stood beaming at them, they both flung their arms around him in a four-handed bear-hug.

'How did you find us? Where have you been? What did you do?' The children talked over each other in their excitement.

'Well,' said Ranjubaba, stroking his beard modestly and twirling a stray dreadlock into place,

'I was in deep samadhi. And then – it came to me. *Dukha!*' he cried exultantly, dropping down and scooping up a handful of soil. 'My rootedness in the Here and Now of Mother Earth was blocking my path to Right Action! It all made sense!' He opened his fist and let the dirt trickle down through his fingers. It made no sense at all to the children, but Ranjubaba had never let that stand in his way. 'So preoccupied had I become with the roots, I forgot the shoots! The flowers! The FRUIT! I channelled my prana through my nadis, unblocking chakras and... in plain English,' he concluded, 'I was worried about you.'

He gathered them back into a hug and shook his head sadly.

'I should never have left you on your own. Can you ever forgive me?'

The children reassured babaji that he was completely and utterly forgiven.

'In fact,' said Jose, beaming. 'This is for you,' and he took out a seed from his tunic pocket and handed it to Ranjubaba.

'No!' he exclaimed, his eyes as wide as saucers. 'It cannot be! Ya'Allah! Oh my god! Baap re baap! Is it? A shraddha beej!?'

Mishi and Jose grinned at him. Then Jose put his hand back in his pocket. 'Look,' he said. 'We've got lots!'

After Ranjubaba had finally stopped Ya'Allahing and Baap-re-baapping, Jose quickly related all that had happened after he'd left them. The notyeti lair (which elicited another round of 'Hai Rams'), the cave, and how they'd found the eternal spring. And then the sleigh-ride down the mountain and how they'd discovered that plasticators had captured the notyeti (Jose tactfully skipped over the part about Mishi wanting to be plasticated herself), and that now the mother and baby were both in terrible danger. When Jose had finished speaking, Ranjubaba drew himself up to his full height and threw back his shoulders.

'Children,' said the old man solemnly, 'as Sri Krishna said to Arjuna on the plains of Kurukshetra: inaction is also action! We have no choice! We must do battle! It is our dharma. There's not a moment to lose. Wahooo!'

Now, Jose was not all that well up on his Hindu mythology, but he seriously doubted whether Krishna actually said 'wahoo'. But he understood the sentiment exactly, and he scrambled hurriedly after Ranjubaba as the old man leapt and bounded down the hillside towards the Dam.

Mishi caught up with them just as Ranjubaba was about to burst into the clearing. 'Wait!' she cried, grabbing his loincloth.

'Aha!' he whirled around, his eyes alight, 'you want me to do battle "skyclad"? So be it!'

'N-no!' said Mishi, alarmed, and the children looked the other way as he retied the cloth around his middle.

'Then?' he said.

'There's too many of them,' said Mishi. 'Just look.'

And Ranjubaba looked – at the watchtowers, the men, the Dam, the Plastication Unit, the crates, the cranes, the diggers, the guns – and even he seemed to realise that there was no point charging in, seedpods blazing.

'Hmmm. I see what you mean,' he said slowly. Then he sat down, folded his legs into lotus position and closed his eyes. 'I will open my Third Eye,' he announced, 'and dazzle them with the Fire of Shakti.'

While Ranjubaba attempted this – to absolutely zero effect – the children sat beside him and pondered their options. That didn't take very long: there really didn't seem to be any.

Then Jose had an idea. In a low voice, as though thinking out loud, he said, 'Maybe what we need isn't more light, but more darkness.'

He explained his idea to Mishi.

'It'll never work,' she muttered.

'Oh, come on, Mishi,' he urged her, 'you can do it.'

'It's different in school, I've never...'

'I know you can do it,' he said, with more certainty that he felt.

Mishi chewed on her thumbnail worriedly. 'Okay.' She got to her feet. 'I'll try.'

She picked up a stick from the forest floor and began to wave it in the air, her brow furrowed with concentration. Slowly, infinitely slowly, white wisps started to appear in the night sky. She squinched up her eyes and blew out her cheeks. She waved the stick some more, as though conducting an invisible orchestra. Clouds thickened on the far horizon, gathered and grew until they blotted out the stars.

'It's working, it's working!' cried Jose.

Mishi whirled and danced, the stick pirouetting about her as she dragged the cloudstuff towards them like a gymnast twirling lengths of ribbon. The air around them stilled and thickened the way it does when there's a storm approaching. Mishi threw down the stick and began waving her arms. Pulled by her outspread fingers, the clouds descended, rolling down from the mountains and pooling into the valley in a thick, soft carpet, and slowly the forest, the Reservoir, the Dam and the Plasticorp construction site disappeared in a rolling grey sea of fog.

'Aha!' cried Ranjubaba, opening his eyes. 'See! I have called down the Cloud of Unknowing!' He sprang to his feet, immensely pleased with himself. He beckoned to the children and the three of them made their way gingerly through the fog.

As they approached the construction site, they could hear voices calling out in the darkness, and vague shapes looming and disappearing out of sight. The searchlights did nothing but turn the darkness into an impenetrable sheet of glaring white, and they were hurriedly switched off.

'This way,' hissed Mishi, and Jose and Ranjubaba crept along behind her, heading for the crates near the plasticator.

They froze, flattening themselves against the side of a crate, at the sound of approaching boots. Then they heard voices.

'...can't see a bloomin' thing.'

'Strange weather, that's for sure...'

'Witchcraft – I'm tellin' you. 'Snot natural. Gives me the...'

'Yeah, I know, gives you the creeps...'

And then the voices and the crunching of boots were swallowed up by the fog.

Ranjubaba peered around the front of the crate and was almost knocked flying as something small and furry and very, very pleased to see him leapt onto his head.

The little notyeti had been hanging around the crates, trying desperately to find a way into the one that contained her mother. She had managed to escape notice by hiding on top of the crate where the workmen couldn't see her, but when the fog descended, so did the baby, to hang upside down, grasping the big steel handle with its toes and bouncing up and down. It hadn't budged an inch (she was a very small notyeti, after all, and it was a very big handle) – and it was just at that point that she'd spotted some very familiar dreadlocks and realised that help was at hand.

'Okay, you. Let's get your mummy, shall we?' whispered Jose, and he was reaching for the handle when Ranjubaba grabbed his hand.

'Wait! You cannot liberate the notyeti!'

'He's right,' said Mishi. 'You'll start wanting to have a picnic or something.'

'Oh no! But how will we get her out?'

'Take Mishi. Get as far away from here as you can,' said Ranjubaba, 'and leave the rest to me.'

'But the minute you open the door, you'll forget what you're doing!' protested Jose.

Behind his shaggy beard, Ranjubaba broke into a wide smile. He rooted around in his bag and came up with a garland of small sky-blue flowers. 'Himalayan speedwell,' he said, his eyes twinkling. 'Guards against the effects of procrastin for up to twelve hours.' He slipped the garland over his head and tucked it securely under his nose like a floral moustache. 'They are also very pretty.' Jose looked at him with renewed respect. Ranjubaba really did know his plants.

'Now – get to the bottom of the Dam as fast as you can. I can only release the notyeti once you are out of range.'

Leaving Ranjubaba at the plasticator, Jose and Mishi made their way through the fog. Although it was still quite dense, there was a definite breeze starting up, and as they hurried along, they noticed that it was beginning to lift the clouds. With each passing minute, the blurry shapes were getting sharper. There was no time to lose.

Suddenly Mishi ducked down, pulling Jose with her. Two large workmen came clumping out of a door and stood looking around.

'Better get the lights on,' said one.

'Yeah. You take the Eastern Tower. I'll get the others.' They split up and headed off in different directions.

'Jose,' said Mishi urgently. 'The control room.'

He looked where she was pointing: the men had left the door ajar. Without another word, they headed towards it.

The children snuck inside and clicked the door shut behind them. After the misty darkness outside, the harsh glare of tubelights made them squint. They found themselves in a long, narrow room with windows along one side, beneath which stretched a console dotted with blinking lights, LED displays and monitor screens.

'Right,' said Mishi, pushing up her sleeves. 'Plasticorp wants to fix everything? Well, let's fix *them*.'

She ran along the control panel, hitting buttons, cranking dials, flipping switches. Then Jose spotted a large metal wheel at one end. He grabbed one side and Mishi grabbed the other, and they heaved and heaved and span the thing around as far and as hard as they possibly could.

Outside, a siren stared to wail. Red lights above the door flashed on and off. And, far below, at the bottom of the Dam, the sluice gates started to open.

'Come on! Let's get out of here,' Jose cried, and they ran for the door, wrenched it open and fled – slap-bang into the two returning construction workers. The children knocked them flying and carried on running as fast as they could, across the yard, out of the compound and down the gravelly slope on the far side of the Dam.

They heard shouts behind them.

'The spy! It's that spy! There she goes – and there's another of 'em! Oi!'

The men scrambled to their feet and set off in hot pursuit – but they had scarcely reached the edge of the site when...

'Hang on a minute, what's the hurry?'

'Wh... we have to...'

The two men looked at each other, puzzled.

'What's that smell?'

'What's that sm... oh, it's...um... ooh, it smells like...'

'Chocolate cake!'

'Nah, more like... I dunno, sort of lemony, with a hint of...'

'Yeah, yeah. Like spicy but sort of sweet.'

'I could do with something spicy but sweet. Ages since lunchtime.'

'My mum used to make this fantastic drizzle cake.'

'Lemon drizzle? My favourite. Here, fancy a game of cards?'

And the two men sat themselves down happily on the ground and started to deal.

As you've probably guessed, while the children were busy in the control room, Ranjubaba had managed to get the crate open, and the baby notyeti and her mother were in an ecstatically hairy embrace. The huge notyeti rampaged around the site wafting great pent-up clouds of procrastin-laced scent in her wake. Everywhere, workers were stopping what they were doing and, despite the fact that alarm bells were ringing, sirens wailing and red lights flashing across the valley, started to chat, amble about and fix each other's hair. Dexter J. Tannenbaum came rushing out of his office to find out what was going on. He stared, aghast, at his men wandering about aimlessly, took a deep breath to start yelling – and then his eyes unfocussed, a kindly look spread over his handsome face, and he wandered over to where two men were sitting on the ground. 'Ooh,' he cried, clapping his hands together, 'Uno! I *love* Uno. Can I play?' And he did.

The children, meanwhile, were running pell-mell down the slope, skidding on gravel and rocks, skinning their knees and smashing through the undergrowth. They finally made it to the bottom of the Dam – but there was no way they could get across to the other side. The floodgates were fully open and the waters of the River of Time were already swirling and roiling through the gorge.

Jose and Mishi set out along the riverbank. They looked back to see if anyone was after them, but nobody seemed to be. The fog had completely blown away, and the night sky above was again strewn with stars, sparkling like diamond dust against the velvet blackness of the night. And there, high up on top of the Dam, silhouetted against the glare of lights, a strange figure capered madly – his dreadlocks were swirling like wild snakes, and in his hands he twirled a garland of flowers like a lasso. Above the roaring, rushing sound of the water they heard a faint, familiar cry: 'Fly children! Go with the flow! Wahooooo!'

The children leapt and scrambled from rock to rock, following the course of the river. They didn't have a choice: there was no way across what was, by now, a raging torrent, and the slope behind them was far too steep to scramble up. The further they went, the stronger the current, the higher the river and the narrower the gorge. They clung onto overhanging branches and stepped from boulder to boulder. The water foamed and crashed, plunging wildly around them.

There was a large flat-topped boulder that Jose could just jump across to. 'Here,' he said, reaching out a hand for Mishi, as she stood on a smaller rock behind him. 'You'll have to jump it. Take my hand.'

'I can't,' she called to him. 'I'll fall.'

'No, you won't,' he said.

The waters were rising around her. Her feet were already soaked. 'Come on, Mishi. I'll catch you.'

Mishi's set her mouth in a determined line and gathered her strength. She took a flying leap.

And fell.

'MISHI!' Jose scrambled to reach her, but in doing so, his foot slipped, and he, too, tumbled into the cascading water. The children were swept along in the torrent, flailing their arms, Jose struggling to breathe each time his head came up. Then he spotted a fallen tree, a little way ahead of them. 'Mishi! Grab it!' As the rapids swept them along, he managed to reach a branch. He hooked one arm over it and stretched out with his other hand to catch Mishi as she was about to be swept past him.

They clung to the tree for dear life, the water tugging at them, pulling at their clothes like a wild beast. Jose's arm was hooked through the Y of the branch, but Mishi couldn't reach it. She clung to his arm, her body buffeted by the force of the current. 'Hang on, Mishi, hang on!'

The water was almost up to the trunk now, fretting and fraying against it in white-capped waves, breaking against Jose's back and soaking his hair. He couldn't feel his arm anymore – it was even deader than the rest of him. He watched, horrified as Mishi's fingers started to slip. 'Don't let go!'

She was clutching his wrist with all her might, but the current had her in its grip. The tree was now almost submerged. Jose grabbed Mishi's hand and hung on, muscles screaming, as she streamed away from him like a flag in the wind, but finally it was too much. Her fingers slipped from his, the raging river took her, and she was lost to sight.

Jose hauled himself up the branch, scanning the foaming waters frantically and calling her name. He clung to the tree as long as he could, coughing and spluttering as the water rose higher and higher and finally swallowed the tree trunk, the branches, and the boy – and swept him downstream.

Dawn was breaking. The river gurgled gently along a wide curve as birds began to sing. It was nothing like the roaring, raging beast of the night before: gentle ripples lapped the grassy banks and played with the tips of the willows as they hung down into the clear water. An emerald dragonfly chased its mate across the limpid surface as a little school of fish darted beneath.

Jose would have surely drowned, but as the river carried him out of Kozitsthereistan and through the foothills, he had stopped breathing again, leaving him safely dead. The water carried him along, rolling him gently along like a piece of driftwood, before finally deposited him on a small pebble beach on a bend in the river and continuing on its leisurely way.

The boy lay motionless as the light grew stronger and the air grew warm with the touch of the sun. Finally his eyes flickered open, and he slowly hauled himself up on one elbow. It felt like every single molecule of his body had been battered, like he was just one giant bruise. He stood up shakily and felt his tunic pockets – they were empty. The seeds must have been swept away as he was spun and tossed in the wild water. He looked around desperately – there was no sign of Mishi. He walked up and down the sandy stretch next to the water, calling her name until his throat was raw.

It had all been for nothing.

The seeds were lost – and Mishi was gone.

Jose fell to his knees in the shallow water at the river's edge and howled. Hot tears undammed, he sobbed his heart out, adding salt water to the river's sweet. He cried as if he would never stop. But finally this storm, too, passed, leaving him limp and empty.

The sun was rising and he slowly became conscious of its warmth on his back. His eyes flickered open and he stared unseeing at the dancing water, the ripples of light on the backs of his hands, the pebbles on the gravelly riverbed. And there, lodged in the space between two smooth round stones, lay a single white seed. Jose waded in, bent down, and carefully plucked it from the water between his index finger and thumb. Then he straightened up.

What was the point, he thought to himself, gazing at the seed as it lay in his hand. This useless little thing had cost him the one person he needed, his most precious friend. He closed his fingers fiercely around the seed until it dug painfully into his palm, and wished with all his heart that he had her back. He felt a black, cold tide of despair rising up in his veins. He pulled back his fist and made to fling the seed as far and as hard as he could – and then he stopped.

High, high up in the pale tangerine sky were two shapes, coasting the thermals on wide outstretched wings. He stumbled out of the water, transfixed, as they spiralled down, soaring over the hills, swooping low over the tops of the trees, and finally landing in a graceful glide on the sandy bank.

'Hey keed,' said El Condor.

'Look who we found,' smiled Perveen. And off her back slid a small girl, a little damp around the edges but grinning like a maniac.

'Hello,' said Mishi. 'You'll never guess. I flew on a *vulture*. It was *awesome*.'

Jose didn't know whether to hug her or hit her. So he took her by the shoulders and shook her hard. And then hugged her like his life depended on it.

'Ew,' she said, pushing him away. 'You're all *wet*.'

'You don't say,' he said, and tucked the single seed back inside his sopping pocket.

As they sailed over the foothills and back towards the school, Perveen told them about how, when they had discovered that the water in the river was flowing again, she and El Condor had set out, flying upriver as far as they could, scanning the forest for any sign of the children. Perveen had first spotted Mishi being swept downstream. They had plucked her from the raging waters, and had been circling for hours when El Condor spied Jose on the riverbank and they flew down to get him.

The journey up to Kozisthereistan, which had taken them days of arduous trekking, was covered in just a few hours flying back. Sooner than he thought possible, Jose felt themselves losing height as El Condor and Perveen flew out of the myst and began to descend in a series of long, lazy spirals down, down, over the great, shimmering expanse of Lake Lachrymosa. Already the water had risen by several feet. The mud around the edge that had lain cracked like old porcelain had disappeared beneath the crystal water, and little wavelets lapped the edges of the grassy banks, catching the light and tossing it back to dance on the underside of leaves. The lake had lost its metallic glaze and was transformed into a shimmering, undulating expanse of liquid light, full of movement and life.

Jose clung on to El Condor's ruff as they swooped low over the water. The vulture tilted to one side slightly to dip the tip of one wing into the water, touching his reflection in a brief salute. As the shining wake of ripples disappeared behind them, he stretched his neck forward and let out a great honk of joy, and Jose laughed with sheer exhilaration.

They finally came to land near the base of the Eerie, and Jose and Mishi clambered down to stand next to the vultures. El Condor stood tall and stretched out both wings. Then he engulfed Jose in an enormous embrace and from underneath this feathery tent, Jose heard his deep voice – a little croaky with emotion – say, 'Jou did it, keed. Jou did it.'

And then Perveen said softly, 'Oh my...'

El Condor unwrapped his wings and Jose emerged into the light to stand next to Mishi. He followed their eyes and looked out over the lake.

In the centre of the lake was a strange churning, as though something beneath the surface was sending ripples radiating out, stronger and stronger, roiling the water into waves. And then, suddenly, a huge dark shape broke free, hauling itself clear of the water, smashing its great wings against the surface and bursting upwards into the air, trailing droplets in a glittering curtain from its feathers. And then another. And another – and another. The centre of the lake was alive with vultures – White-backed, Bearded, Egyptian and Black; Hooded vultures and White-rumped vultures; Turkey vultures with crimson heads, King vultures wearing ermine cloaks; magnificent white Himalayan vultures with long black wing tips; Griffons and Condors – their harsh, joyful cries filling the air as they burst clear of the water and headed towards the Eerie.

When the last of the birds had hauled itself free, and the waters of Lake Lachrymosa were once again smooth, El Condor turned to Jose his eyes shining.

'Jose. Keed. How can we ever thank you?' he said, overcome with emotion.

Before Jose could to reply, Mishi said, slowly and clearly, in a voice not quite her own, 'You can take him back to his family now. He wants to go home.'

El Condor cocked his head at Jose, an unreadable look in his eyes.

Jose looked at Mishi as she stood there, her eyebrows drawn together in a dark line, her lower lip caught between her teeth. He could see that she was trying to be brave. Then he came to a decision.

'I'm not going,' he said.

She looked up, startled. 'Wha…? But you want to – you said. And the lake's open now, so…'

'I'm not leaving you,' he said. 'I lost you once, and I can't do that again.'

Jose reached into his pocket and brought out the seed for them all to see. As he looked at it, sitting there in the palm of his hand, he realised something that he had, perhaps, known all along. There was no going back for him – there never had been – but if there was one thing in the whole world that might – just might – help his mother to carry on, to move forward into a future without him in it, it was this: a seed of hope from the River of Time. His heart broke a little, but it felt to Jose like this was only because his small body was too small for such a big feeling. It broke, but not to shatter – it broke *open*.

He turned to El Condor.

'Your Excellency?' he said.

'*Sí, mi compañero.*'

'Will you... could you make a very special delivery?'

El Condor's ugly beak split into a wide smile. 'Of course.'

Jose gave him the address, and the big bird stretched out his crooked neck and took the seed carefully in his beak. Then he crouched low, took a lumbering run and launched himself into the sky. Perveen, Mishi and Jose watched as El Condor Pasa, Supreme Commander of the Cathartes Aura, Lord of the High Thermals, Conquistador of the Raging Storm, Guardian of the Sacred Updraft, climbed high into the misty sky and then tucked his great wings into his sides and plunged down like a missile into the shining waters.

Jose looked across the lake to where the familiar silhouette of twisting spires and upturned roof tiles cut into the grey skyline. Gravepyres was waiting. It was time to get back to school.

'Do you think we'll be rusty-gated?' he said.

Mishi nodded. 'Definitely,' she said.

*I*n the weeks that followed Jose's death, there had been a steady stream of visitors to flat number 23, Dilshad Garden. Friends, neighbours, relatives. Mr Srinivas's parents had flown in from Chennai, and his father had rearranged the living room, putting dhurries and cushions on the floor for people to sit on, as they had soon run out of chairs. Mrs Srinivas senior had draped a small coffee table with a white cloth on which she had placed a framed picture of Jose. It was a school portrait, taken in his last term, and he was wearing his blazer and a bright blue tie. He was looking slightly back over one shoulder, straight at the camera, his hair uncharacteristically oiled and neat, combed flat to his head. He was smiling, as he had been told to, though his eyes were focussed a little beyond the camera, as though he'd noticed something just behind the photographer's head. The plain black frame was draped with a garland of crimson hibiscus flowers, and on either side candles were kept lit day and night. 'No priests,' Mr Srinivas had told his mother, so she visited the local temple every morning as was her custom, and offered up her prayers there. He did not object when she returned to the flat with cardboard tubes of incense, and the air was fragrant with sandalwood.

Padmini Aiyer came by with freshly steamed idlis and a tub of green coconut chutney. 'Her favourite,' she whispered as she handed it over, as though Mr Srinivas didn't know. Mr Aziz from number 52 arrived each morning with hotpots full of rogan josh and chicken biryani that he had made himself, each more spicy and delicious than the last as though, if only grief could be doused with sufficient cardamom and black pepper and cinnamon, it would melt into thin air. The dishes joined the others in the small fridge until no more tubs and cartons could be squeezed in, and Mr Srinivas finally resorted to giving them away to the family downstairs who did their ironing, to the mali who looked after the colony garden, and to Jamal and Sheela, who came to cook and clean. They took the food with heavy hearts, and when they sat down to eat later, with their own families at home, the meals tasted subtly different. Perhaps it was some unknown spice. Perhaps it was sadness. Or perhaps it was just a surfeit of love that found it had no place to go.

Jose's mother lay in the bedroom, with the curtains drawn and the door closed. She had scarcely moved since that terrible day, and had hardly eaten a thing, and then only in listless response to her husband's gentle coaxing. She lay unmoving in the hot darkness, staring up at the whirring blades of the ceiling fan as day turned to night turned to day, each as flat and featureless as the last, her ears stoppered to the wailing and crying on the other side of the door, until they, too faded away and the flat lay silent again. Her brother and sister-in-law had scooped little Surya up and taken her to stay with them, where she could play with her cousins – while her mother lay dry-eyed on the bed. Her limbs felt like stone, and the seconds ticked by leaden and slow.

As another day dawned, traffic rumbled past, honking and belching, buses careened along tootling their shrill arpeggio horns, auto rickshaws rasped as they wove in and out of the stream of cars. The vegetable-seller trundled his cart along and called his wares up to the balconies and windows: 'Tamatar-mataar-aloo-brinjaaaal'. The familiar shush-shush of stiff brooms filled the colony's lanes as sweepers piled the dust into small brown hillocks in the gutters. Crows quarrelled in the gulmohar trees and flights of green parakeets shrieked past as the city went about its business under the hot beige sky. The monsoon was late this year, and the heat was relentless. Men and women hurried along to offices, dark circles under their armpits, freshly laundered shirts and blouses already wilting, their skin glistening as though they had just stepped out of a shower. In other words, life carried on as normal, seemingly unaware that for Mrs Srivinas it had already ended.

Then clouds began to gather on the horizon, and there was a metallic tang to the air. The sun wrapped a cloak around itself and disappeared, plunging the city into shadow before night had a chance to fall. Beneath the roar of traffic, a deeper rumble sounded in the distance: thunder.

Padmini Aiyer threw open the window in her kitchen and looked out over the colony park, inhaling deeply. Mr Aziz packed his spices away and stood out on his little balcony among the pots, his hands deep in the pockets of his kurta. In Shalimar Bagh, Surya and Jose's aunt shooed the little girl and her cousins out into the lane to join the neighbourhood children, who were already whooping and playing in the cooling air, while from the roof terraces kites tugged against their strings, their swooping parallelograms bright against the dark sky.

Then the first swollen drops fell, knocking dust off the leaves and peppering the sandy heaps in the gutters. The pavements were quickly polka-dotted, and as the downpour intensified, they were spattered with dark wet circles that sizzled as they fell, one after the other. Soon the lanes were black and shining, the air intoxicated with petrichor. The rain quickly thickened to a torrent. Lightning flickered behind roiling purple clouds and burst through in forked spears hurled at the earth.

The rain played a deafening drumroll on corrugated iron roofs, lashing through trees that bent low before the wind. Children ran back home trailing muddy footprints in the hallway, and in the tea shacks and roadside snack stalls the owners added fistfuls of ginger and extra sugar into bubbling cauldrons of chai.

Unseen, above streets that had already turned to wide brown rivers, a dark shape flapped through the rain. Head hunched back into his body and eyes narrowed, El Condor flew into the wind, scanning the glittering city beneath him. The streetlights were on, and cars nosed their way through the water, headlights sharpening the raindrops in their white glare.

Suddenly a huge crack rent the air, lightning lanced down and found its mark. A shower of white stars burst overhead as a powerline came crashing down and plunged half the city into darkness. Generators sputtered into life and a few lights flickered on inside apartment buildings.

Still holding the seed carefully in his great beak, El Condor spiralled low over the houses, his keen eyes sharpened for cables. He ducked down beneath the tangle of black lines and landed on the wet earth outside flat number 23. He placed the seed carefully on the ground, and as if on cue, a stream of water overflowed the guttering from above and cascaded down. For a second the seed just lay there, a glowing white moonstone, and then as the shower of brown water swept over it, it sank quickly into the mud. The great bird shook his feathers, sending a shower of droplets into the air. Then he nodded his head and, satisfied, heaved himself into the air on powerful wings and disappeared into the darkness.

Mr Srinivas pushed open the door to the bedroom and stepped carefully into the dark. 'Leila?' he said, as he carefully put down a tray. A form stirred on the bed. He put a hand on her head and gently smoothed the hair from her brow. 'I have made some kitchuri for you.' She lay for a while, her hand in his, and then slowly began to sit up. Mr Srinivas arranged the pillow hastily behind her and then placed the small bowl of rice and dal on her lap. She took the spoon and her husband held his breath, as though the smallest movement might break the spell.

She took a mouthful and chewed slowly. And then she looked up at his kind, weary, worried brown eyes, so like those of their darling boy, and the corners of her mouth turned ever so slightly up in the beginnings of a half-smile. And then she spoke the first words to have left her mouth since that wail of raw grief so many weeks before.

'Too much salt,' she said.

Jose's father leant forward until his forehead touched hers, and they sat together in the darkness, adding a little more salt to the bowl between them and listening to the rain fall.

As they approached the school, the children could hear the sound of the Chant Memorius floating out through the windows. They slipped in at the back of the hall, while everyone's eyes were closed, and sat down cross-legged with all the others. With a ting of the bell, the chant faded to a close, and all the children stood up to go.

When Madam Morte saw them, she seemed neither surprised nor angry, but simply ushered them out along with the rest. Jose and Mishi looked at each other, nonplussed. Maybe they wouldn't be rusty-gated after all.

As the day wore on, it began to seem that not only would they not be punished, but that they hadn't been missed at all. Maybe it was something to do with what happened if you nearly drowned in the waters of the River of Time, Jose thought. Who knew? He was just happy to have escaped unscathed.

Instead of going straight to the Study Hall that evening, the transitioners were summoned back into the Great Hall for a special assembly. The teachers were all lined up on the podium, either side of Professor Yama, who stood tall and aloof, wrapped in his black cloak, his silver scythe resting on the lectern beside him. When everyone was settled, he started to speak.

He started by thanking them all for their diligence in chanting the Golden Sutra, morning and evening, every day. 'The Chant Memorius, as you all know, is a chant of great power. We knew that it had helped to sustain Lake Lachrymosa in these recent troubled times, but thanks to Madam Morte's excellent suggestion' – here he turned to her and gave a little bow, which she modestly returned – 'that we increase the frequency and intensity of the chant, we are pleased to announce that the lake has returned to its former glory.'

There was a burst of chatter among the assembled children, and the monks and nuns turned to each other, beaming and patting each other on the back. Once the applause had died down, Professor Yama resumed.

'It is indeed something to be thankful for,' he said. 'A miracle, even. As I always say,' and here he looked straight at Jose, with a twinkle in his eye, 'a little hope goes a long way. Now, in celebration of the fact, I am pleased to announce that there will be no homework today. In fact,' he went on with a sweep of his hand, 'no homework until further notice!' The hall erupted in cheers and whoops as the transitioners leapt up and stamped their feet with approval.

The Deadmaster's surprise announcement did not, however, extend to lessons. The next day, there was a full timetable of Scare Studies, Entropology and Cloudforming before break, and double Mathamythics straight afterwards. Jose was still rubbish at Cloudforming, and Mathamythics continued to baffle him entirely, but he surprised himself – not to mention Madam Morte – with his progress in Scaring and even managed to quite enjoy Seeing with Dr Chiplunker at the end of the day.

He went with Mishi to the library to check out the next in the *Magic of Acornland* series so she would have a deadtime storybook to look at, but when they came to horizontal, the book lay forgotten and their two candles burnt low as they sat together talking about everything that had happened. They talked about Ranjubaba and the notyetis, and wondered what had happened to Plasticorp and the smooth-talking Mr Tannenbaum when they discovered what the children had done. The Dam still loomed large in their imaginations – they hadn't managed to destroy it, of course, and the floodgates could be closed and the mechanism repaired. Still, they had managed to get a temporary reprieve for the lake, and for the moment at least, that was more than enough.

As the days went by, Mishi seemed to slowly revert to her former, forgetful self. One day, as they were sorting through the grosseries at Houri McClury's shop, Jose said, 'I wonder if "Baba Black Sheep" is still scared of spiders,' and Mishi looked at him like he'd lost his marbles. 'That's Little Miss Moffat, silly,' she said – and Jose realised that she had forgotten it all.

Jose felt a little sad to think that he was the only one in the whole world who now knew about their quest beyond the myst and into the mountains of Kozitsthereistan in search of the Eternal Spring, and he vowed to himself to remember twice as hard, since he had to remember for them both.

Not long after they had returned to school, or perhaps it was months or years – Time's a slippery thing in the Land of the Dead – Jose was sitting in class when a perfect came in. She had a quiet word with the teacher, and then signalled to Jose to follow her out.

'Professor Yama wants to see you,' she said, when they were outside the class.

'Me?' squeaked Jose. 'Am I in trouble?'

The perfect said nothing and led the way to the Deadmaster's study.

'In here,' she said. Then she rapped smartly on the door and walked off.

'Come in,' came a deep booming voice.

Jose pushed open the door and stepped inside.

Professor Yama was standing with his back to him, gazing out of a tall narrow window. As Jose came in, he turned and smiled. 'Ah, young Jose,' he said, and gestured to the rugs on the floor. 'Sit, sit.'

Jose sat down and crossed his legs. Professor Yama flicked back his cloak, folded his long legs, and sat down facing him. Lit from behind by the window, Yama's white hair framed his ebony face in a sort of halo. The old man and the young boy sat facing each other for a while, until Jose, fidgeting, cleared his throat and said, 'You wanted to see me, Sir?'

'Ah, yes,' said Professor Yama. 'Yes, I did.'

He pulled a scroll from the folds of his cloak and held it open in front of him. Then he searched around in the other side of his cloak before finally finding a battered old spectacle case. Seeing Jose's look of surprise, he smiled ruefully as he put them on. 'What to say, Jose. Even the god of Death can be a little short-sighted.' Then he peered at the paper.

'It seems to me that you have been doing rather well,' he said. 'Seeing, straight As. Scare Studies, Exceeds Expectations. Mathamythics, good. Entropology, good. Your hard work does you credit, my boy.'

212

'Thank you, Professor,' mumbled Jose.

'No more melancholia? What about homesick?' he said.

'N... no,' said Jose. 'Not really.' And it was true, for although he had far from forgotten his previous life, and there were still days when he ached, positively ached to be back in Delhi with his mother and father and little sister, he found he could think of them with a love that seemed to fill his heart to the brim but without overflowing.

'Good, good,' said Professor Yama. He carefully rolled up the scroll and tucked it back in his cloak. 'Well, everything seems to be in order and I've had a word with your teachers and they all agree. You are ready to take the Exitamination.'

Jose looked at him, stunned.

'Report to the Great Hall tomorrow at the third gong. And be ready.'

Time flew by and then it dragged its feet. Each second seemed to be waiting for the next to arrive, but before he knew it, hours had passed and the reverberations of the third gong ricocheted off the wooden columns and echoed around the courtyard. The old tree in the courtyard stretched its twigs, gave its needles a little shake and settled back into itself. Transitioners streamed out of the doors and into the main entrance, making their way in chattering groups into the Great Hall. Up in the rafters bats chittered, and the pale grey light through the stained glass fell in colourful patterns on the stone floor.

Professor Yama sat impassively at the front as the children filed in. Around the edges of the hall, teachers sat in their yellow robes, each with a white silk scarf draped around their shoulders. The school scaretakers were there too, sitting on one side. The children fell silent as the monks began a low rumbling chant. Two of the nuns got up, walked slowly to either side of the podium and slowly drew aside a richly embroidered tapestry that hung on the wall behind Professor Yama's head. As the tapestry was parted, it revealed a huge stone carving of a snake that formed an unbroken circle, its tail in its mouth. The snake's scales were mosaic tiles of turquoise, gold and red, and one obsidian eye glittered black in its head.

The chanting ceased and a hush fell over the hall.

Professor Yama rose and stood with his scythe in one hand, the wickedly sharp blade curved above his head like an inverted new moon. Everyone stood up.

'We are gathered today,' he intoned, 'to call the Chosen to the Exitamination. I shall begin.'

As he read out each name, one transitioner after the other made their way to stand with Professor Yama at the front. 'And lastly, Joseph Eapen Srinivas.' Professor Yama looked up and scanned the room. Jose sat frozen to the spot, unable to move. Then he felt a sharp jab in his ribs.

It was Mishi. Or Mishi's elbow to be precise.

'That's you,' she hissed, her eyes wide and excited. 'Go on! Go on, then!'

Jose stood up unsteadily. He looked around. There were his classmates – his friends – and Professor Chiplunker with his mad glasses, Madam Cecelia and Madame Morte, and Houri McClury and the young librarinun, both smiling at him, their eyes

215

shining. And there standing beside him, elbow half-bent to give him another jab if needed, was Mishi.

He remembered her voice, echoing around the mountains as she called after him: 'You can't leave me…'

As though he could read his mind, Professor Styx came over and gently put an arm around Mishi's shoulder. 'She can't go with you, Jose,' he said quietly. 'We need her here. The new transitioners would be lost without her.'

And Jose finally understood Mishi's desire to be plasticated: it seemed like a way out, for a girl who had none. He looked at her toffee-coloured eyes and she smiled at him, and he realised that in a day or two, or maybe three, he too would fade for her, like the whole amazing adventure already had, and that she would forget him completely, and that would be fine.

And maybe one day she'd run across the courtyard and grab some other kid's hand and say, 'You're *late*. Come on.'

He looked at her, his Forever Girl, and knew there was nothing left to say.

Professor Yama beckoned him to stand with the other chosen ones, and he took a step towards them, across the empty space.

Jose followed the other chosen ones as Madame Morte led them down a corridor he'd never been along before until they reached a door at the end marked 'EXITAMINATION'. Jose stood silently at the end of the line as one by one, they were called in.

The line dwindled until only Jose was left.

And then it was his turn.

Madame Morte held the door open for him and he walked through.

It was pitch black inside, and he stopped short, wondering how it was that the light from the corridor hadn't penetrated the room at all. He looked back at the door – it was still half-open but the light stopped dead at the edges, as though it was a painting of a doorway and not the real thing at all. The moment that thought popped into his head, the doorway disappeared and he could see nothing, nothing at all. He took a step forward.

'Hello?' he said. It was silent as the grave, and so dark he didn't know if his eyes were open or shut.

'JOSEPH EAPEN SRINIVAS,' a voice boomed. A voice that was made up of many, many voices – deep, high, old, young, all speaking as one.

'Y-yes,' stammered Jose. His knees felt very weak.

'YOU HAVE BEEN CHOSEN,' the voice went on. 'ARE YOU READY TO TAKE THE EX-AM?'

Truth be told, Jose had never felt less ready for anything in his life, or death for that matter.

'Okay,' he said in a small voice.

'YOU MUST ANSWER ONE QUESTION AND ONE QUESTION ONLY.'

He swallowed.

In front of him, as though projected onto a screen, a piece of paper appeared. It was an ordinary, perfectly blank sheet of white A4. It hung in the air, glowing faintly and moving ever so gently, as if wafted by a slight breeze.

'TELL US,' the voice intoned again. 'IS THE PAPER FULL OR EMPTY?'

Jose thought hard. Everything he had learnt at Gravepyres had led up to this. But nothing, nothing from Scare Studies, Mathamythics, Seeing, Cloudforming or Entropology–nothing had prepared him for this: a black room, and a sheet of white paper.

He stared at the empty page. Was this a trick question? The page looked blank, but what if it was actually full of invisible writing? He squinted at it harder. No. There wasn't the faintest indentation on its surface. It was definitely...

'Empt...' And then he stopped.

Professor Styx's strange remark came back to him, that day as they sat by Lake Lachrymosa: 'Learn what you must, unlearn what you think you know.' Jose felt like he'd been handed a key. The only problem was that he had no idea what it was supposed to unlock.

One thing that he *had* learned at Gravepyres was that nothing was quite what it seemed, that six plus four didn't always add up to ten. So if the page looked empty, the answer must be that it was...

'Fu...' he started to say. And then he stopped again.

He stood alone in the darkness and the silence, staring at the page while long, slow moments passed. A strange notion came upon him that the page was looking at him, just as he was looking at it, like a woodland animal caught unawares. It almost quivered.

He narrowed his eyes and thought about the paper: not what it was for, not what writing it might contain or not, but the paper itself. Where did it come from? Wood pulp. But where did that come from? Wood, obviously, which in turn came from trees. In his mind he pictured a forest – rustling leaves, birdsong, lemon-yellow sunlight filtering through. And what were trees made of? Water and sunshine and earth. And what was sunshine made of? Bits of light: tiny, tiny specks of energy that couldn't even be seen. And water? Salt tears, dewdrops, molten ice, solid steam... and earth was spider's silk and millipede feet and grains of rock and fungus, pollen and old seed cases and mothwings and worms and dead leaves and animal bones and people and... and...

Everything, absolutely everything.

The paper was not separate from anything else. Nothing was! Words could not exist without the spaces between them. Sound could not exist without silence, grief without love. His mother's anguished cry and her tenderest lullaby could not exist one without the other. He would not exist without his parents, and they without theirs, and his grandparents without theirs, back into the farthest reaches of time. Time itself could not exist without matter to change and alter. He remembered being tugged and tumbled through the waters of the river unleashed by the Dam, that feeling of being drowned and overwhelmed and yet held up and carried along in the powerful flow. The paper was full – it was so obvious!

But was it empty of anything?

All of a sudden, he had the answer. But how to put it into words?

'The paper is both full and empty,' he said in a clear voice. 'It's full of everything. And it's empty –' he hesitated, choosing his words with care, '– of being separate. Of being separate from anything else.'

At that, the edges of the paper began to dissolve. The whiteness of the page danced with the darkness, and the darkness danced with the light until there was no edge, no separation between the two, just a continuous shimmer of pulsating stardust. Jose looked at his hands as they, too, began to lose their outline in a haze of radiance. His body seemed to fizz with tiny fireworks, filling him with helium lightness. Streams of energy blazed out through every hair on his body, until the boy known as Joseph Eapen Srinivas ceased to be separate from anything else – and became full of the universe.

He had Passed.

EPILOGUE

Professor Styx closed the book.

'Again, again!' said Mishi.

It was Mishi's favourite deadtime story – an 'extra-special book' given to her by Professor Yama because, as she always said with a touch of pride, she had 'extra-special needs'.

Professor Styx smiled at the little girl who was lying under her shroud, knees bent, her eyes catching the candlelight and her face shining. He knew that every time they opened the book, she would have forgotten how the story ended, and each time they got to the end, she had forgotten how it all began, and so they would have to start all over again.

He cleared his throat, turned to the first page, and began to read.

'You're late...'

EPILOGUE

ACKNOWLEDGEMENTS

Sometimes it seems that thanks are never enough, and blessings too numerous to count. So: to the very many people who have helped me to find my way through the Land of the Living and without whom this strange story would never have made it to the light of day – my lifelong, and quite possibly eternal, gratitude.

First and foremost to my brother Sanjoy, for believing in Jose, trusting in Mishi, and having faith in me. This is his story as much as mine. To my amazing niece, Polly Rodgers, for laughing and crying in all the right places. And to her dad, Ranju, for letting me borrow his name for one of my favourite characters: he's one of mine too.

Parts of the book were dreamt up, written, discarded, re-written and edited in some very special places. Thanks to Miranda Bevis for the shedlet, to Jay Griffiths for her gazebo, Michael Watt for his kitchen table, and mum and dad for their greenhouse. Thanks too, to Arshia Sattar and the dancers of Nrityagram, for a wonderful writer's retreat at Sangam House in Bangalore; and to Mita Kapur and Kunzang Choden, for inviting me to the Bhutan Literary Festival where the story had its first fledgling flight.

I am blessed to be part of a community of writers, both in India and England, whose feedback, editorial acuity and emotional support have helped me immeasurably: thanks to Nilanjana Roy, Rana Dasgupta, Samit Basu, Annie Zaidi, Mridula Koshy, Nisha Susan, Parvati Sharma and all the good folks of the Riyaz writer's group in Delhi for their patience, their laughter, and for putting up with my terrible puns; to Anil Menon and Vandana Singh for giving me the courage to write; to the peerless Karthika Naïr for more than I can possibly say; and to Urvashi Butalia and the rest of the Zubaan gang for allowing me enough string to go fly this particular kite.

To Lionel and Jo Ward at Brendon Books in Taunton, and to Maya Crook, my young friend and 'ideal reader', thank you. And I cannot forget Richa Jha, who first set the Gravepyres ball rolling, and Sarah Odedina who, perhaps without knowing it, kept it going. And to my editor, friend and publisher extraordinaire, V.K. Karthika, for the leap of faith.

I would like to acknowledge the fantastic work done by the conservation consortium known as SAVE (Saving Asia's Vultures from Extinction), and the staff and volunteers at the Hawk Conservancy Trust for allowing me to meet their magnificent vultures at first hand. El Condor and Perveen would be proud of you.

Writing is a slow and solitary process and without the people who kept the house going, the kid fed and cared for, and the plants watered, it just wouldn't have been possible. Naga, Sangeeta, Mali-bhaiyya, and so many others: thank you so much. And without the precious and ever-present friendship of Amit Mahajan and Juhi Saklani, I don't know what I'd have done. Bless you.

ABOUT THE AUTHOR

Anita Roy was born in Calcutta, grew up in England, and lived and worked in Delhi for twenty years. Her mother is English, her father Bengali, and her life has been a happy mix of cultures.

In 2004, she founded the Young Zubaan imprint for children and young adults, and was one of the founders of the Bookaroo Children's Literature Festival. She is the author of several non-fiction books children, and her stories have appeared in anthologies such as *Superhero!* and *Eat the Sky, Drink the Ocean*. As a freelance editor and writer, she contributed extensively to the international bestseller, *Goodnight Stories for Rebel Girls*. She is also a regular newspaper columnist and book reviewer.

She is the author of *A Year in Kingcombe: The Wildflower Meadows of Dorset*, and holds an MA in Travel and Nature Writing from Bath Spa University. *Gravepyres School for the Recently Deceased* is her first novel.

She lives in a small town in southwest England with her son Roshan, and Alfie, their cat.

www.anitaroy.net